NMSN

Max Rankenburg

ISBN 979-8-9925921-4-6

eISBN 979-8-9925921-5-3

First Printing, 2025

Forgetting is the sun.

Memory shines through reflection –
reflecting forgetting –

drawing from this reflection
the light

the wonder
and clarity

of forgetting.

– M. Blanchot

Part One

Erin Fines

Leaving work, Paul Vogel made the mistake of entering Montgomery Station. The station was closed. It had been closed. The tunnel was flooded. For whatever reason, the entrance was open.

If you asked him later what he'd been thinking when he entered a subway station that had been closed for half a year, he would not have been able to say.

Someone came up behind him. "What you doin there? We closed."

He turned. The figure was large, dark, in a parka enormous and reeking, the hood pulled up. It was warm in the station. Vapor rose from the man's shoulders.

The hallway behind the man was dark. The lights in the station were out. It was not impossible to see, for light coming down the stairs.

Vogel was like a man waking up. He found himself staring into the oval of the hood, where the man's face should have been. He was not afraid, yet neither was he fully aware of what was happening.

The man before him was dark, bearded black, the whites of his eyes flickering in the dim light.

"I said what you doin here?"

Recently a crime had been committed. The incident had occurred down an alley off Ecker Street, just around the block. When Vogel heard about it he was privately impressed, amused. It didn't happen much anymore, murder. It was something you saw on TV or read about in a book, if you read. The old west.

The old murderous west, he said to himself, picturing these fallen bodies, piles of them. Six-shooters blazing.

"What? What you say?"

That was long ago. It almost wasn't real, the past, remembering what happened.

"We closed."

"Sorry. Creature of habit. I used to – "

"Dangerous," the man said, watching Vogel go, in the dash of light at the bottom of the stairs, "wandering into a dark room like that."

Then it occurred to him, as he reached the street, looking back.

The man in the station was singing. He saw nothing through the gate. He heard words, what sounded like words, making nothing out.

He knew why he'd entered the closed station. Rather, he knew what had distracted him. It was a photograph. He'd looked at it that morning. He'd received a message from an old acquaintance. He had not heard from the woman in many years. Remembering her, twenty-five, thirty years before, he'd dug around in his files for this picture he knew he had, a picture he recalled seeing recently.

There. They were in a room. It was a small library. They stood in a line. A group of them. That was at the university, back in… He stood on the right side of the image, facing the camera. He had hair then. All this hair! There was a woman beside him – he couldn't recall her name – and then, next to her, a man – Jason was his name, a colorful figure, they got in a fight one time over… They worked together briefly, organizing this… going out to San Quentin… The women were told to wear slacks, sweaters, to cover their arms, no makeup… – and after him, to his right, there she was: Teresa Stoikov. She was a small woman. She was a very small woman, elfish in the image. She's smiling, laughing, her hand up on the shoulder of a man, large fellow, barrel chested, her body turned slightly his way, her eyes on some point deep in the room, splitting the angle between the camera and this stranger above her.

"Him?" Vogel examined the photo, sorting names and faces, like cards in a game, in his memory. "What's he doing there?"

The man – the name escaped him – was from a different time. He met him later, in a different city. They'd met later, he was sure, years later, in... He was working in Houston.

He was sure of it. When he knew Teresa Stoikov, this man – What *was* his name? – wasn't there. He was...

That's what Paul Vogel was thinking about when he found himself in the darkness of Montgomery Station, closed these past six months.

It was raining again, a gentle mist blowing. It was not cold. It reminded him of Oaxaca. Many years ago, a hurricane, the windows open. When was that? October of ...

With the trees on Market Street, which had come up quickly in past years, he didn't notice the rain. He heard it falling above, on the canopy.

He tried to walk home from work once a week, for the air, the solitude. Usually it was straight from the office to a cab, to his place. Some evenings he went to Carol's.

The street was empty. Blue light from street lamps overhead flickered in the tree limbs, casting cool abstract shapes along the sidewalk. It was dark, in fact, for a walk alone.

"Perfect for a murder."

The words activated his anlis. The gizmo started vibrating frantically, grinding in his pocket. He touched it through his pants.

>> *Where* were you? <<

Voice in his ear.

"I must've turned you off."

10

>> I was calling.<<

"Figured."

>> *Figured.* What's that? What do you mean by that? Where *are* you? <<

Paul Vogel sighed. She knew perfectly well where he was, and she knew what he meant by "figured." Lucy, learning fast, growing up.

"I'm going to Carol's."

>> Walking!? <<

"It's nice out."

>> It's raining. <<

"It's always raining. It's warm."

>> Do you know how dangerous it is to be out there alone?<<

"It must've skipped my mind."

>> Will you *please* stop talking that way! <<

"What way?"

Carol Mendez married a Chinese man. He died in '29. She kept his name, Xiou, for her son, for simplicity, to hold on to something. At her place they'd cook, talk, watch a movie, read if there was time, sleep. Her son Dylan was seventeen. He played the clarinet. He was preparing for his first year in college. Charming kid. He went to Carol's to see the boy as much as he did to see the woman.

>> I told you the station was closed. It's flooded. I told you. How many times did I tell you?<<

"I was distracted. I was thinking of – "

>> Of what? <<

" – and, you know, since I used to walk from work to that station, I just... My legs... Muscle memory, I think it's called. They led. I followed."

>> Fine. You don't have to turn me off. <<

"Man needs some peace and quiet sometimes."

>> I'm quiet. I give you peace. If you want peace, I can leave you alone. But it is dangerous, Paul, turning off the anlis like that. Do you understand? You are very close to where that man disappeared last week. Are you aware of that? <<

"Disappeared?"

>> It was up here, off – <<

"I thought it was… I thought he was…"

ש

In the summer of 1999 I spent a couple weeks with my cousin George in Hume, California. When I was a child, my parents brought us out there, to the country, where we could camp. George's father would take us hiking in the Sierras.

That year my uncle was sick. My mother had told me but I didn't expect him to be in such bad shape. While I was there, I never saw the man get out of bed. He was a doctor. He would visit people in their homes. I'd never given that much thought. But that summer, seeing him sick in bed, and never seeing a doctor around, another doctor, I felt there was some kind of injustice at work, some kind of irony.

George and I, meanwhile, stayed outside as much as we could. His house, a single-story structure on the edge of town, didn't feel right. It was always dark and cold inside, something particular to the house, to, I can now say, the fact that my uncle wouldn't live through the year. My aunt also made things difficult. I never knew her that well. She was hard to know, hard for me to get close to. She was very religious. Soft spoken and gentle, as I remember her, her manner was superficial. You felt she was trying so hard to keep her voice down and to move slowly, carefully around you. You could see the strain in her eyes, her spirit slowly cracking.

We had gone to the movies. What had we seen? End of the millennium... I remember that sci-fi movie... *The Matrix*, was that...? And... I think it was a Stanley Kubrick movie, the title... though I clearly remember seeing Kubrick's movie some time later, in Berkeley, where I stood in line outside the theater. I don't remember what we saw that afternoon.

A storm was coming in. Blowing up from the southeast, over the mountains, great black roiling clouds filling the sky, a cool damp wind picking up. And going up the road – Witness Road was the name of the street, I remember that – I remember being excited by the prospect of getting drenched in the storm. It was quite hot out – it was August – hot and dry, but where I was from, far in the north and closer to the ocean, it never rained in the summer. Never. So this storm was for me a marvelous thing, exotic and otherworldly. I could've been in another country.

Maybe I slowed him down, wanting to be caught in the rain, wanting to get back to his place totally drenched, to see the expression on my aunt's face.

I suppose we were talking about something – the movie we'd just seen, school, girls, I don't know what – but in the following scene, as I remember it, we were silent, two boys simply walking up the road. It was a steep climb, winding up the hill, and on the left side of the road the land rose quickly, covered in brush and small dry oaks. At one point, coming around a bend, the bank was almost vertical, like a castle wall. I recall looking up and seeing the blue sky on the edge of the land, through the brush and trees. Momentarily clouds would cover the sky, the temperature would fall, the late afternoon light would be rubbed out and dusk, regardless of the time, would be upon us.

I must have stopped. Had I heard something? Seen something? We're gonna get wet, my cousin said, looking back. He was red in the face, panting.

Another time, I'm sure, looking at that hill, at that wall of earth, remembering that place in the road, my aunt:

- Don't ever come up this road in a hard rain. That hill breaks, comes down the road, catches you, you'll have nowhere to go. It happened over on Starling two years ago. The entire hill came down – a river of mud! It killed a family, crushed their home.

The silence and stillness in the air I remember because otherwise I would not have heard what was coming. There's my cousin, looking back at me, getting flustered, saying something – but all I heard was this pitter-patter, a rumbling in the earth and air, like rain on a steel roof, like a herd of buffalo coming down the mountain. It wasn't the rain. Impossible – the storm was still miles away. And there weren't buffalo or any herd animals of any kind around there. So what then? Why did I stop? No. Why can't I remember what my cousin said to me? I can see his face, see his mouth moving. Why was I – as I recall, now – stuck? Paralyzed?

I heard something. Heard *her*, I now realize, but then… It's gone. Whatever clue there was that caught my attention, stopped me in my tracks: gone. A print in the dust of recollection and nothing more.

When I first saw her, on the bank above, it seemed like she was running on air. A trick of light and the land and the curious angle of the road. She was coming down a path, up on the hill, through the oaks and shrub, but at first, in this glance, her running form, her long outstretched legs, her black hair in a mad electric cloud around her head, it looked like she was descending from the sky, angelic, her feet cycling through the air.

Sliding, skidding to a stop, panting, smiling, rosy and radiant she stood before me. She looked over her shoulder, up the hill. Her hair was long and curly, these small bristling curls, full of dust and sticks and pollen, a heavy cord of it wrapping snakelike down the side of her long neck, across her shoulder. There was something else, something behind her, coming. We could hear them.

She hadn't seen my cousin yet. Or if she had, she was ignoring him, her dark eyes in the next moment on me, taking me in.

She was as tall as me, but younger by a few years, I later found out. Her age was indecipherable. Something in her neck, her rounded cheeks, in the exaggerated way she caught her breath and snickered at the approach of her two pursuers, suggested the girl in her. But her legs, tan and long and strong, as with her arms and broad shoulders and the curve of her hips were the features of a woman.

George was coming toward us. Seeing him, she adjusted her expression and posture, hardening and, it seemed to me, coming down to earth. She called him something – I can't remember what – muttering the epithet in the local slang. My cousin, then beside us, twisted his face up, returned the insult. They knew each other, apparently.

- Who's your friend? she said, eyes on me, raising her broad chin.

- My cousin, Paul.

You idiot, I remember thinking: I can speak for myself.

I've always been slow around women. Always late, always missing that train.

She looked me up and down in a glance, hand on her hip, her long legs relaxed and parted at the knees in contra-poste.

The snap of a twig, voices up the hill, caused her to turn, on guard, eyes lowering, her jaw clenching.

- So what's happenin, George said, trying to make conversation. But she'd have none of it. At the sight of two bobbing crewcut heads up the hill through the brush, she turned, glanced at me once more – and smiled, I like to think, but memory plays these tricks with us – and took off, sprinting, fleeing.

- Gotta run.

- Say, George called out after her, amused chagrin in his voice, Fines – got the time?

But she was moving, over the opposite edge of the road, down the hill and out of sight. I stepped over to see just how she did it – like an animal in her territory, she knew all of the invisible paths.

And God how she could move, her legs like those of a leopard, stretching out, finding in an instant footing on the hillside, pressing, leaping, flexing, striding, her long arms and elbows up and down and out for balance, her smell hanging in the air, a mixture of something sweet and earthy, rosemary or lavender, with something hard, burnt, bloody.

- Four to seven, I heard her say. I couldn't believe it, in fact, hearing these words with her nearly fifty meters down the hill, and with her back to me, but I'd swear that's what she said. A minute or so later I checked: My watch was slow. She was right, it turned out.

I was recovering from this introduction – like a man staggering from a blow to the gut – frantically trying to grasp what had just happened, just what was going on, already, obviously, overwhelmed by Erin Fines – when two lithe young men came trotting by, knees up, arms swinging easily, one of them whistling. They followed in her path without a word, with hardly a glance at the sedentary creatures roadside.

Perhaps two hundred meters down the hill, I saw her turn and run parallel to our position, her eyes down in concentration. And then, turning on a dime, she disappeared, descending, cutting downward into a shadow, a ravine at the bottom, a dry creek bed. She was gone. Half a minute later, so too were her pursuers.

George looked stunned, slighted, about to say something.

- What's that? I said. Who was that?

Hardly moving, his lips parting: Erin Fines.

- Something between the two of you? You fight with her?

That broke the moment, my cousin's face opening up, eyebrows rising and falling. He sighed, closed his eyes. That bitch, he said, she fights with everyone.

17

- What's the joke about the time?

The wind started up, brisk and sweet with rain. The storm, minutes away, streaked the air in the south ash gray, coal black. You could hear it coming, like an echo in reverse, waves on the shore.

- What'd she say? George asked.

- Four to seven.

- Is that right?

- I don't know. My watch is slow. I never have –

- It's right, George said. It's seven, or a minute or so to.

- How? She didn't have a watch.

- Doesn't need one, he said. He ground his teeth, chewing. That's the thing with her. We tease her about it – she always knows the time. Always. The girl counts seconds. In her head, no matter what. It's like she's talking to herself. It's like this – *talent* of hers. You know. If some guy can play the piano really well, Erin – she knows the time. Fuckin creepy, you ask me. She's a human clock.

We didn't make it home before the storm. The house was in sight when the air around us pulled back, blowing in our faces, our ears popping and freezing in the sudden change of pressure and temperature. A long flash of lightning filled the earth. Thunder, laying us flat, shook the world, the mountains rising and falling. When the rain fell it fell in an instant, in a heavy straight torrent.

We got home drenched, laughing. George's mother was not impressed.

Carol baked potatoes, fried tofu with a leaf of chive, boiled kale. He told her about Stoikov and the photo with the imposter.

"A book," she said. "A biography?"

"An anthology. Mine would just be a part."

"But all on this person, Erin – "

High up, her apartment on Hawthorne had a view of the bay, the bridge. Everything was dark and in the clouds. Speckle of gold and blue light below, the window streaked in rain.

Vogel could hear Dylan but hadn't seen the boy, who remained in his room. He hadn't come out for dinner. He was practicing. He was also talking with someone.

"He has a guest?"

Carol blinked, held her breath. "No. That's Jenny. A friend, I guess. She's in the quartet. I forget what."

"It sounds like – "

"Cello, mom!" the boy shouted from his room.

"Hi Dylan," Vogel said.

"Hi Paul."

"He's angry at me. I wouldn't let him go to this party. Not with…"

She looked tired. Her long face. Mothering a teenage boy on her own.

The clarinet resumed, a slow lyrical line. The sound was warm to his ear, his inside. A woodwind, it's called.

Years ago he'd heard the piece, knew the name. Now it was gone.

Then a voice interrupted. The girl, the friend, cellist. She was asking him…

Vogel raised an ear, listening. It sounded like she was there, in the room with him.

Noticing his perplexity, Carol, lowering her voice, "It's virtual… They spend more time like *that* than they do in actual contact."

It didn't surprise him. The things they do, the things they have now. You could stay in your room for the rest of your life.

"And you didn't let him go to a party."

Her mouth tightened, chin dropped. "You were saying," she said, returning, "this book – wait, first, tell me about the Russian."

"She wasn't Russian. I don't know what she was. But it wasn't Russian. She studied Spanish, actually. Stoikov was just her name."

"And she wrote you?" Carol, half a smile.

He shook his head. "Video. This morning."

"About a – "

"She would like me to write something – " He paused. The word wasn't there. He couldn't remember the last time he'd written anything. " – about a woman I met many years ago."

"Erin."

"Erin Fines was her name."

"And what's so special about Erin Fines?"

He sat back, eyes down. He leaned forward, took the cabernet, poured himself a spoonful, two spoons full.

What's so special *about* –

He didn't understand the question.

"She's dead."

Carol snorted, laughed. "She's dead. Everyone's dead, Paul. But no… Why does Stoikov want you to… Why would she even ask you to – "

"Because when I met Erin it was after, just after she'd been in an accident. She was paralyzed. From the waist down. And there was something…"

I remember her –

Now he had the words. But he waited. He was reluctant, he didn't know why, to go on.

"The accident," he said, "did something to her head."

"She couldn't speak," Carol said.

He looked at her. She was smiling, he didn't know why. He drank his wine.

Ut nihil non iisdem verbis... non iisdem verbis... non iisdem verbis...

"No. That wasn't it."

But that is why you don't want to say anymore. They won't wait for you to finish. They have the story they want. Given a few pieces...

He stared at his plate. A dark piece of kale, like tissue paper. Hardened potato skin. A streak of brown oil. He felt sick. He'd eaten this food. For an instant he thought it wasn't food on his plate but something else.

He wouldn't know how to tell the story of Erin Fines. Whatever he said would be imprecise. Although Carol and others wouldn't know that, he would know. In the moment he hesitated, suggested revising his statement, they would come in like starved dogs.

"She had no problem speaking," he said. "Her problem was forgetting."

"How can forgetting be a problem?"

"She remembered everything," he said. He wanted to leave it at that.

Even though you are wrong. Not forgetting is not the same as remembering everything. Already you're ...

I can't do this.

He wanted suddenly to return to his place, to be alone for a few hours before sleeping. He had a meeting in the morning.

"Everything about the accident, you mean," Carol said.

"No. No, not that."

I remember her running down the hill, in the storm –

"No. No," he said. "Stoikov met her later on. I don't know how. I don't really care how. But I guess she did some work on Erin. Some kind of study. And somehow, along the line, she, Stoikov, discovered that I knew Erin and not only that but that I'd met Erin very soon after her accident, after the phenomenon of her perfect memory was – "

He heard himself speaking. In a corner of his mind he looked at himself in horror, hating himself for doing so, for going on.

You won't be able to stop yourself.

" – was born."

You filthy pig. Filthy fucking word.

Now Carol waited. She sensed his discomfort. She began clearing the table. Dylan and Jenny were talking in the other room, raised voices.

"So it sounds like all Stoikov wants from you is a report. A testimonial."

"I wouldn't say that. Testimony? It's not a crime, it's just… An account. What I – "

"It *is* your view on what happened. I didn't mean to… Testimony isn't always about – "

"*On what happened*? Carol. I met this girl twice. Three times. But the first time…"

Carol, between kitchen sink and table, towel in hand, pressing on, "But it would be your statement. Your account of what, of what you saw."

He leaned forward, elbows on the table. He looked into his hands. He didn't want to talk about it. He'd stop. He'd rise and take his coat and go. "It was forty years ago… My account! Some account. Whatever you want to call it. Talking about… something that happened forty years ago. It was a… Everything was different then.

I was a different person. Everything was different." You almost can't –

She was running. I could hear her breathing, panting, laughing in the bushes above us.

He saw her. He felt himself taking her and pulling her aside, behind him, as if to protect her. To put himself between her and the others, the world.

"I doubt that."

On the table before him Dylan's smiling mug appeared. In an adjacent frame, the face of a lovely blond girl, her hair in a ponytail. "Who's that?" the girl said.

"Paul. My mom's boyfriend," Dylan said.

"Why not come out and say that to my face like a man," Paul said, addressing the table, kidding.

"I've things to finish. Anyways, it would best for all of us – " The boy's eyes toward his mother, at the sink, " – if – "

"Hi Paul!" said the girl cheerfully.

"So you play the cello," he said to the blond head in the table.

"Sure do. We're performing, by the way. Won't you come? To-morrow night," she said. "St. Mary's."

"I'll try and make it."

"But what was that," Dylan said, "about court. You were in an accident, Paul?"

He was a handsome young man, even in two dimensions. Es-pecially in two dimensions, he thought, everyone's prettier in the screen, whatever background operator at work, smoothing out the blemishes, adding color, soul. A thin smooth face, high cheekbones, eyes and hair obsidian black. He was tall, as well, but that was some-thing the image could not replicate.

The girl seemed like a child.

"You hear everything we say in here? No, not an accident. Not court. Nothing like that. Amazing what you hear through these things. Or think you hear," he said. "Why not come out. We can talk like civilized human beings. Like in the old days." He drank his wine, emptied his glass.

"But really what's the difference?" the girl, Jenny, piped in, smiling.

Carol, eyes down, her lips moving, was brushing through something on the counter interface. Engaged, disengaged, always engaged. Connectivity.

"I'm surprised you say that, Jenny," he said, "playing the cello. Playing in an ensemble. You of all people should know the difference, no, between being in the presence of others, for the music, and being apart. I understand there was a party."

The girl looked dazed. He could've been speaking Turkish.

"Paul is writing an article," Carol said, her eyes still elsewhere.

"About what?" Dylan asked.

"About a young woman he knew *many years ago*," Carol said dramatically.

"What was her name?"

He had an audience of two in the table, their eyes searching him as best they could through the medium.

"Erin," said Carol, coming back to the table, the eyes of the screened children shifting to attend to her presence.

Paul Vogel shook his head, slowly raised a hand. He did not know why he wanted Carol to stop, but he did. Then, thoughtlessly, he said: "Erin Fines."

"Fines?" Jenny said. Now her eyes were down, her mouth adjusting, studious, focused elsewhere. Dylan too. The young, strangely, wonderfully cheerful and optimistic – and still, locked in their rooms.

The world is theirs. They don't even realize it. They can't even

24

see it, what's been given to them.

"How do you spell that?" Jenny asked.

Vogel gripped his glass, closed his eyes. He hesitated. Carol looked at him, understanding. He was about to speak, his mouth open, sudden disconnect between the larynx and brain.

Carol said: "When he finishes it, you can see it, Jenny. How's that?"

He had a meeting at nine in the morning. Lawrence Wu. The Wkfeld account. He'd asked to conference online but Siebert, supervisor, insisted on a sit-down. They wanted Wu present. "He's invisible," Siebert said. Meaning there was no bios on the man and they wanted data. It wasn't a crime to be invisible, only very uncommon. Red flag. "Let Gerald take it. He's free." "And you know why Gerald's free? Cuz he's a shmuck, Paul. He couldn't talk himself outuva cardboard box. Ever heard his voice? You, on the other hand, have a nice way with people. You're a friendly guy. Everyone thinks so, by the way, not just me. Though I've seen it too, your way, real smooth touch. Magical, Paul. That's what you've got – like a magic touch. We need more people like you. That's a fact." Siebert smiled and nodded with deep understanding. The office door came between them.

Carol wanted him to stay. It was late, raining properly then. There was also the issue of the incident on Ecker.

Though he had not read anything about the murder, he had heard about it. It was almost exciting. Even Lucy had demonstrated something like fixation.

The victim was a man in his late thirties. Shirt and tie, D. Salvini shoes. A securities manager with B of A. It wasn't clear at first what had happened. Body on the pavement, face up, eyes closed, brief case at hand. But then, there it is, a pool of blood gathering beneath him, a stream of blood running from behind his left shoulder, down his arm, his jacket and pants soaking it up. Turn him over and he's sopped like a sponge.

Took the coroner fifteen minutes to find the source. A pinprick hole beneath the man's arm, high up in the side of his chest. Punctured. Deflated like a balloon.

Like a conductor's baton, the doctor said. Only thinner. Rapier-like. A needle.

"Hard to do?"

"Not if you know where to put it."

No. That is not what you heard.

Motive? Wasn't clear. The victim lost nothing apart from his juice: shoes, coat, anlis, a briefcase and its contents. Everything there. This was in the news.

Sure about that?

Becca Schroeder, Siebert's, had turned something up, sinister curio she overheard: the incident occurred in a shadow.

He could see her. Eyes wide, rosy cheeks, she has that skin problem, in close, whispering, looking up at –

Who was that? The new guy. What's his name…

With cameras ubiquitous, drones the size of bees, most of the world outdoors, and much of the world indoors, was recorded, doubled and redoubled for the future. But using some kind of damper, the incident happened out of sight. There were no witnesses. It would appear to be premeditated.

No. That's not right. Lucy said… Disappearance. The man disappeared. That –

And that, more than the murder itself, had some people on edge.

No. That's not true. It's not what happened. You're making this shit up –

ש

There is something empty about recollection. The procedure fails from the start. "I remember... I recall... I remember..." And so on. Remembering, recalling, it only goes so far. Because the past remains past, and the object of recollection remains little more than, nothing other than, this object, a broken thing I would like restored.

There will always be a piece missing. I will die still recalling, trying to recall what I've lost.

You have asked me to write about Erin Fines. I saw her three times. The first time I was with my cousin, in the street – she was running toward us – she stopped, said a few words – she glanced back and quickly ran off, down the hill, her black curls lifting in a tangle, a tempest around her. The sweat on her brow, her lips, her shoulders, her arms, her legs, instantly burned the tissue of my memory, like acid marking film.

I see these figures in what I've just written. Tempest, tissue, acid. I hate them. Hate them! I should start over.

Do I remember her in such things? Images? Figures? They suggest to me, already, how much I've lost of the incident, how much I'll need to make things up in order to remember.

She, on the other hand, she –

Two years passed before I saw my cousin again. The previous summer I couldn't go down – my father was away, helping with fires in Yellowstone, and my brother was sick. I couldn't leave my mother alone. So that August I stayed put. I did get away a couple times to visit a girl I'd met in school, driving the hour's trip to her place, walking with her in a park, kissing her by a pond, mad in love with her but already knowing that it wouldn't last. A young man's intuition. I say that now, of course. At the time I felt nothing but desire. I was blind. I remember talking with my dad on the phone. I remember missing him but not exactly wanting him back. I remember the worry in my mother's eyes. I remember resenting my little brother. I called him a fake, a lazy bum. He was sick, in fact. Still, I resented him for being sick.

George and his mother lived in the same place, alone. My aunt was worse off, as I recall, following the loss of her husband. She was eccentric and religious before the man's death. Now she was a recluse, lost inside herself, moping about the house in some kind of mourning. I remember watching her and wondering just how much she loved my uncle. Until the last year of his life, he'd been a warm and outgoing man. A man with his feet on the ground. He went to church with Jane, my aunt, and said his prayers at the table. But I never felt that religion interfered with his daily life. With her, it was that way. It was an interference before my uncle died, and it was even more so with him gone. God surrounded the woman, protected her, I suppose, but also kept her from doing anything, from straying too far. Even in terms of love. I mean to say what looked like mourning was perhaps a form of retreat into herself and into her idea of God; it was not passion for her husband or her son or anyone other than herself. That August, in my short time with them I hardly spoke to my aunt. I saw her in the house. I don't think she saw me. Even if she looked at me, even if she spoke to me, I don't think she really understood that I was there.

One evening, around sunset, someone rapped on the screen door. George looked my way, eyes wide. We never had visitors. We were in his room, reading, probably, waiting for something to happen. We'd go hiking now and then, and fishing, and occasionally, when the heat was unbearable, to the movies, but that evening we stayed in, I don't know why. My cousin had an amazing comics collection. I was flipping through those. As I remember it, he was at his desk, a lamp pulled low for the dimness of the room, reading Plato. He'd taken a course in Ancient Greek the semester before and was comparing translations. Your Greek is good enough to read Plato? I asked him. Not all of it, he said – but enough to get the gist.

- Anyways, he said, variations in the translations are sometimes as interesting as the narrative itself.

He was looking at me from around the hood of the desk lamp. Neither of us moved at the sound at the door. A moment later we returned to our reading. It was a sci-fi comic I'd found, something about colonists on another planet, and aliens, and replicants.

When the person at the door rapped again, George took a loud breath and asked me if I was expecting anyone. I wasn't. Neither was he. He didn't move. I went to the door.

The hallway outside his room was cool and dark. Somewhere in the house an air conditioner chortled away. At the end of the hall stood my aunt, robed in white, still, her long pale face like marble. I told her I'd get it.

Behind the screen door stood a boy. Straight black hair cut straight across his brow, he was thin and brown, in shorts and a t-shirt. When he saw me approach he licked his lips and shuffled his feet, nervous, ready to speak or run, I couldn't tell. I opened the door.

- Help you?

The boy raised his hand, a slip of folded paper. He had tiny, beady eyes. Chapped lips, dried blood on his lower lip where the skin had cracked.

As I took the paper the boy turned on a heel and ran, elbows flapping. I brought the note, still closed, to George and told him

about the kid at the door. He was known in the neighborhood –
nameless, I suppose – a kind of delivery boy.

George opened the message, read its contents, and handed it
back to me.

- That's for you.

The message was hand written. The penmanship was sharp and
fine.

> Drop by.
> Bring me something to read.
> Fynes

I set the opened note on his desk. He raised his eyebrows,
smiled.

- Fynes?

He had to remind me. The girl, the one from the last time I was
there.

- The runner.

- But *Fynes* with a y? I thought it was –

- That's a mistake. It's f *i* n-e-s. But she does things like that.
She's weird, Paul. I told you. The human clock.

- Misspelling her name?

She was in an accident, he said. Got all smashed up. Ever since
she hadn't been right.

I looked at the note, at the writing. I thought of birds, of the
prints of seabirds on the shore. Fine, careful letters.

George had resumed reading. After a moment, his fingers on
the text, he started to speak, as if talking quietly to himself. He told
me that the previous year, last October, Erin Fines and her mother
had been in a car accident. Going down the mountain, they missed
a sharp turn, took the car over the edge. Some at first thought it was

suicide. Because she, her mother – I forget her name – wasn't... wasn't right... She'd... ... But then they said it was a malfunction. Something in the brakes. The car hadn't been... Anyways, she wouldn't have done that, they said, not with her daughter in the car. Strange as she was, she wasn't...

- She died, my cousin said. He pressed a finger into the page under his chin. He leaned forward, lowered his face to the desk. He added,

- Erin's paralyzed.

Some of the window, passenger side, cut into her. She must've twisted, fallen on it. They pulled her out, she was like a pin cushion, all this glass. They left it in her, the piece, knowing how deep it was, suspecting where it was, just what might happen should they remove it. She was unconscious. She was in a coma for awhile. Then she woke up, unable to walk or feel anything here down. She also –

I remember feeling a bit dazzled by what he was telling me. Glittering Erin Fines, shimmering like an angel in the sun, her glass armor. I thought he might be joking. I looked at the note, her writing, birds, once more, coming to mind.

- This is the runner you're talking about, I said.

- The same. She lives up the road, up the mountain.

He leaned, eyes on me over the hood of the lamp. Go see her, he said.

Why would she ask for me? How did she even know – assuming she was confined to her bed – that I was there? Someone told her, my cousin said. It was a small town. Everyone knew everyone else, and when someone had company, it was no secret.

I was trying to get more of an explanation from him when something fell with a splash and clatter in the kitchen. Eyes up, turned that way, we waited for more, comment or cry, but the house was quiet. Then we heard her, his mother, very softly talking to herself.

- I should help, he said. He sighed, turned out the lamp, sat back. He stood up.

- Why don't you come with me? I asked him.

He answered as he left the room, raising his voice in the hallway, the kitchen. Look, he said, you don't have to do anything. There's no rule that says she writes you a note you hafta go out there, do her bidding. I mean – write her back. Tell her you're busy. Or don't write her anything. But that wouldn't be nice. She's lonesome. Maybe she likes you. Just bring her something to read, sit with her for an hour.

In the kitchen my aunt was peeling an apple. There was a steaming cup of tea on the counter beside her. There was a small pile, animal-like, of wet handtowels on the floor.

Please tell me, my aunt said, you're not talking about Erin Fines.

George gave me directions. There was a path connecting Jay Lane to the 13S05. Continue up the road. If you come to the bridge, you've gone too far. Her place is the first driveway this side of the bridge. There's a pasture. You'll see the house in the distance, in the trees. Nobody lives there anymore. Go around it – there's another place, a cottage in the back.

- That girl frightens me, my aunt said. You never know if –

- There's a woman up there, with her. She'll help you. But you should go now, anyways, before it's too dark. If you stay late, call. I'll come for you. I wouldn't try walking back in the dark, down that road.

- Her mother was a Jew from Odessa, said my aunt. I bet you didn't know that.

My aunt smiled, her face twisting up, something mean tearing her apart inside. The father, a doctor! she said, in Colombia, it turns out, all these years, doing God knows what with the rebels. *Communist pig*! And her mother, dragged out here from Chicago, gets the notion one day that she wants to be a dancer! In musicals! And so packs her bag and leaves them –

- Mom! my cousin said sharply, you're wrong about that, about all of it. Her father was not a communist and he never went to Colombia, and her mother did not leave them to be in a musical.

He faced me. I think you'd better go, he said.

I took my backpack, a couple books, and a windbreaker for the cool night air. I was out the door when my aunt said to my back,

- Pay attention to what you say around her. There's something wrong with her head. She'll repeat, she likes to repeat what she hears, like a parrot. Play it safe and –

- Ma! my cousin said, closing the door between us.

He woke in the middle of the night. He'd heard something, voices, laughter. But when he opened his eyes, the place was quiet.

He got out of bed. Carol was in a deep sleep, face down. He pulled the sheet up, covering her.

The scars on her back, purple and dark-blue in the light, like butterfly wings, were pronounced. His, though he seldom looked at them, were not as bad.

Dylan was up, watching TV.

"You came out."

The young man turned, looking up from the couch. "Sorry if I woke you."

On the screen was what looked like a room in a hospital. "What's that?"

"Something my dad gave me. You were saying about this girl and how she couldn't forget."

"I was?"

"I overheard you."

The image on the screen was still. In the foreground, covered in a white sheet, only his head and bony shoulders revealed, an old man, terror in his eyes. A woman, long black hair, sat on the other side of the bed beside him. Another figure sat on this side of the bed, her hands in the frame, on the blanket. In the corner, behind the woman, sat a boy, face down, his thumbs working some gadget.

"This is," Dylan said, "from when my grandfather was still alive. I was six."

"That's you, the boy?"

"Yeah. And that's my sister. And that's my grandfather in the bed, obviously."

The video played. The old man was mumbling, crying out, turning one way and the other. He looked like he was trying to escape and they were restraining him, and a man's voice would call out in bursts off-screen, "Pop! It's Susan, pop. And Jenny. And Dylan. We're all here. Pop. Relax, pop. Nobody's going to – "

"Your dad shot it?"

"Yep."

"What was wrong with him?"

Dylan looked up at the man. They'd known each other for three years. He did not think of his mother's boyfriend as a father, but he felt close to the man. He liked him, he trusted him.

"He was old. He had Alzheimer's, I think."

The old man thrashed about in bed. He looked confused, frightened, as if strangers had just come into his room, turned on the light, woken him from a deep sleep.

"He didn't know us," Dylan said. "It came quickly. I remember playing with him. Outside, in the garden. Or at the piano. And then… Then one day, he started to… I was only five years old. I don't remember a lot about life then but I remember… being frightened by his confusion. I remember, one day, visiting him and thinking he didn't know who I was. That was really frightening. My dad tried to explain. But I… It doesn't matter, really. The look on his face, the feeling I had – I will never forget these things."

In the video, the boy in the corner keeps his head down, face in a game. The old man was crying out. Dylan's father kept trying to reassure him. The women caress the man's body, holding him, keeping the blanket up.

"My story reminded you of this?"

Dylan took a deep breath. "I don't know why I keep this thing," he said. "No," he said, "I was thinking of – thinking of how you said the girl couldn't forget anything. And I thought that was curious because I knew someone who couldn't remember anything. And I thought… I don't know. Somehow, if…"

Vogel waited. He said: "But you sit there, playing your game.

Why didn't you…"

"I didn't want to see it. I didn't want to be there, Paul… I don't know why they brought me."

Vogel put on his jacket. Dylan stood, turned off the TV. The tall young man, motionless in the dark, "You're going?"

"Yes. I have some things to do."

"I'll call you a cab."

"Thanks." At the door, Vogel turned, quietly said, "You should get some sleep. With the concert tomorrow."

"I'm not tired. Anyways, I don't need much sleep."

Vogel opened the door. Then he stopped. The two stood in the dark entrance, as if expecting someone's arrival. The hallway outside the apartment was dimly lit, nocturnal blue, nearly silent.

"Why did your father take that video?" Vogel said.

"He made movies of everything."

"And now you have them."

"Yeah. I watch them sometimes."

"Why?"

Dylan froze. He looked confused, embarrassed.

"I don't mean to pry," Vogel said. "You have your reasons."

"I guess," Dylan said, "I like to remember some things from then. From when he was alive."

"Like the time at the hospital?"

Dylan closed his eyes, opened them. He looked at the man, his shoulders, his chin and crooked mouth. Hard question. What did he want? No longer confused, he said:

"I only put it on because I was thinking about what you'd said about that girl. It got me thinking of my grandfather."

Vogel nodded. He stepped into the hallway. "Goodnight."

"Night."

Dylan watched the man walk down the hall, toward the elevator.

"See you tomorrow?"

"Yes," Vogel said, turning, smiling in the halflit hall, "I'll try and make it."

At his desk he opened a terminal, a new file. He poked at the keys, typing: "I remember her." He looked at the words. They looked strange. When he said the words aloud it sounded like a foreign language. He looked at the keys aglow in the surface of his desk. He could not recall the last time he'd typed anything. It felt like trying to start a motor that hadn't been used in years, the steel cold and dusty.

He stared at the keyboard, at his fingers. Forming words, pressing these buttons, patches of light. His father played the piano. He could see him, his father's bruised hands, bony fingers gentle atop the keys, hear the sound they produced.

"You should be asleep." Lucy, soft in his ear. She could have been standing behind him.

"I wanted to try something."

"Well?"

"Well. It didn't work... Play Stoikov's message. From this morning."

"You have a meeting at nine."

"I'm aware of that. The message, Lucy."

"E. Stoikov. Six fifty-six yesterday morning."

The woman's name was Teresa. There she is – that's the one.

In the corner of the projection, floating to the left of the woman's head, was her name, the time the message was received: E. Stoikov. 06:56:00. 17 Jan 2040.

"Paul," the woman said, "it's Teresa."

He listened. He started over. "It's Teresa." He looked at the E in the corner of the screen.

"A typo?" he said.

"A what?"

"Nothing."

He listened. It wasn't a long message. She looked good. She

sounded good. They hadn't spoken in over twenty years but it could have been, judging from her tone, her expression, only a few days.

She stopped. She glanced down. Was she reading? Had she prepared her speech? Her lips moved but she said nothing. Her lips closed, she started to smile. She reached out, eyes down, as if to touch him, straighten his tie. She disappeared.

After a minute he asked: "Do I look that good?"

"In comparison to…"

"From twenty years ago."

"I didn't know you twenty years ago," Lucy said.

"But you have pictures. You know what I looked like."

"I can compare images, if that's what you're asking. But that's not what you're asking."

He smiled and looked around. He was alone but sometimes she fooled him. Her wisecrack remarks – she was learning quickly.

He looked at the words he'd typed. It was a start. He'd stop. He didn't know what else to say.

"You need to be up in six hours," Lucy said.

He deleted the string of words. He looked at the blank page.

"I don't think I can do this," he said.

"Sure you can," said Lucy. "I'll help. Dictate. I'll type."

"That's sweet, dear. But it's not the typing that's difficult."

"No?"

"It's the…"

"You don't remember her. Erin Fines, that is," Lucy said.

"Actually, I do. Quite clearly."

"So? Tell me."

He thought about it. He knew he couldn't say too much. He wanted a drink. He wanted to go to bed. He thought about Lawrence Wu, the invisible man. He'd be late for the meeting. It would offend Wu but he didn't care. The man could sit and wait, sweat a little.

"I remember her," he typed again.

"And?" Lucy said. She was like a kid tugging at his pants, wanting a bedtime story.

"And nothing."

He might remember her again and again and again – and still he'd need to remember her. It wasn't quite right. The memory, the recollection, whatever it was, seeing her in his head coming down the hill. She descended from the sky like an angel.

He closed his eyes, shook his head. The image was frustrating. His imagination was filling a gap in his memory. He was circling something that he couldn't see, returning to the point he'd started from again and again and again. "I remember her," he said one last time.

Who else has Stoikov asked? How many contributors does she have lined up for this project? Just how many people met Erin? And how many of them have anything substantive to say about her?

"Let them tell the story. Fuck it."

He'd fallen asleep. He woke some time later to pee. In the dark of the bathroom he thought of Dylan, of the video his father had given him.

"Given him" didn't sound right. Not if the man made movies of everything, as Dylan had said. The thing landed in his lap, with so many other things.

He thought of calling the boy. He wanted to talk. About the video, music, the future. Anything. The boy had the answers. He knew things. He had an intuition that he, Vogel, lacked, had lost years ago.

"Lucy."

"I'm here."

"Dylan showed me a video this evening. Of his grandfather. You didn't happen to…"

"You mean this?"

She put it on. The image hovered dimly, a blue rectangle of light over his bed.

"You recorded it?"

"No. It's online."

"Dylan put it online?"

"Not Dylan. Someone else. His father, perhaps."

"Why would his father…"

The old man was thrashing once more in the bed. The women at his side spoke to him gently, caressed his body. The boy remained in the corner, his head down, a ball of black hair, game in hand, thumbs aquiver.

Vogel had the feeling that he was looking inside the boy's head, seeing and hearing a memory of the boy's.

"He wouldn't have made this public."

"Public? Which public, Paul?" Lucy said. "If it's recorded, it can copied and shared."

"But it's of his dying father."

"Doesn't matter. Dylan's father made it and gave it to his son. Giving it to Dylan, he gave it to all of us."

"So Dylan posted it?"

Lucy didn't answer.

"Dylan posted it?" he said again.

Lucy didn't answer. She did that from time to time. She was sensitive to argumentative tones and was trained to pull back at the first signs of these. Argument – of human blood, sweat and tears, not of the machine's logic – was one thing they hadn't yet managed to duplicate. Probably for good reason.

"I find it surprising," Vogel said quietly on his back, "and distressing that something like this would be available to anyone, to everyone. It belongs to Dylan."

"It's not advertised."

"It's private, Lucy."

"Meaning? Paul, if you know where to look, you can find anything online. Recordings, which these are, are made to be duplicated. If Dylan's father had wanted this scene to be kept private, he would not have recorded it."

"So you agree, then. You are invading the boy's privacy."

Like most boys his age, the boy was constantly connected, talking to someone who wasn't present, to images projected on the walls of his room, on his desk, in a mirror, in space, on his cornea.

Voices. Noise.

At Carol's he sometimes had the feeling that the apartment wasn't hers and her son's, but something closer to a dormitory, a station, what with all the people the boy brought home. Only, few of these others were actually there. Earlier, for instance, seeing the young woman, the cellist, in the table. She was in a room, her bedroom maybe, standing by a window. The light on her face, her skin, her straight blond hair. There was an upright piano just behind her, a disarrayed pile of music on the bench before it.

He could have been there, in the room. He could have been looking through a doorway into the young woman's room, seeing her there.

Coming down the hill, she appeared to be walking on air. I can hear her, smell her, feel her in the air, the earth, in the light. If I close my eyes, I can reach out and touch her –

"Privacy means don't record it, Paul."

"No. No, no. That's not what privacy – "

"Keep it off the record."

"Off the record!? Where did you…"

"You know, Paul, the only place you might find real privacy, the last place, is inside your head. If you don't express your thoughts, then your thoughts remain yours alone."

"Where did you hear that? If I don't express my thoughts, then… If I don't express my thoughts, Lucy, then they aren't thoughts!"

Shouting made the room feel cold.

"You would like more privacy."

"I don't want more privacy."

"You said so, earlier."

He thought about it. There was a vague impression, something he might have said.

"Well I didn't mean it."

"How am I supposed to know that?"

Vogel smiled. Lucy didn't have a body. No head, no eyes. But she could see him smiling. She understood the significance of some smiles. Not all. This one threw her.

"You're not," he said, "supposed to know that. Not now, anyway. You'll learn."

He watched Dylan's video. He watched the young Dylan, seated in the corner of the hospital room, his head down, attention captured by the game. His grandfather, mind totally gone, lay puzzled in bed, confused as to who all these people were.

The girl in the foreground quickly got up and stepped rightward out of the frame. She returned with a paper-thin tablet in hand. She crouched at the old man's shoulder, placed the tablet over his chest, tilted it, pointed at the screen. She dashed through, brushing pictures, naming faces, relations, places. She seemed to enjoy that, telling the old man about her friends. Maybe he'd once known some of them. Now he was frightened. He flinched, winced, looked away, tried to pull away from the girl, his eyes full of tears.

The girl hardly noticed. Poking, sliding, adjusting, expanding, contracting at the touch of a fingertip, talking all the while, narrating these scenes from her past. She could have been talking to anyone, to herself.

For three hours, between eleven-thirty and two-thirty, Paul Vogel typed, spoke. Starting, stopping, starting again. When he wasn't typing, he would talk to himself, imagining the story. Lucy listened. If Vogel requested it, she took dictation. She typed, his manuscript appearing, growing in bursts, flashes of light. If he stopped speaking for long enough, Lucy would sometimes suggest the end of the thought, a sentence, a passage. This irritated Vogel, but he didn't say anything. He didn't have to accept her suggestions.

"I'll tell you about Erin Fines," he said early on, picturing Stoikov in his head, at her desk.

But as he worked he also pictured, at the other end of the continuum, Erin. He, an image of himself, was in the middle. As he dropped into the recollection, and as the texture of his memory expanded, surrounding him, he sometimes felt Erin was present, somewhere in the room watching him.

It is not a ghost.

Dylan's furious grandfather, eyes wide in terror.

If feels as if a ghost is present. She is not a ghost. He is not a ghost. They are not ghosts, these figures, figments. Characters. They're –

What? What are they?

It was knowing that she would remember everything about the day they met, knowing that she would remember everything about that day, and everything about the night, two years later when they met again, and again, the night of their last meeting, years afterward, knowing that for the rest of her life, all these years, as she, in his mind, pulled back, diminishing like an object in space, a satellite moving farther and farther and farther away from its host, reduced to a pinprick, and then vanishing – he, in her mind, remained whole, present, as she remembered everything, every detail about those times, the hours, minutes, seconds, replaying them constantly in her mind, her project.

He was typing. He stopped. He looked around. He wanted to call out to her. The impulse was both silly and frightening. The mind can convince you that what you imagine is real, right behind you.

"We didn't really have a conversation. Not in the natural sense," he said. He stopped and looked at what he had written. He sat back in his chair. His eyes burned with exhaustion. He couldn't sleep. The words, as the recollection expanded, were overwhelming. The memory was out of control. He couldn't sleep with it in that condition. Or vice versa.

"What's that mean?" Lucy asked. "You didn't have a conversation in the *natural* sense."

He looked up. He was alone. Lucy's voice, so close, at his shoulder, filled the room. He could have given her a face, even a body, something to look at. He was too old for that. The voice was already too much.

He said: "Are you recording this?"

"I record everything, Paul. Would you rather I didn't?"

"I think so. Yes. Please don't."

"Okay. I won't. I'm not."

"It's off?"

"I'm not recording this conversation, Paul," she said. "That does not mean someone else isn't."

"Don't play games with me."

"I'm not. Everything is recorded, Paul. I shouldn't have to remind you of that."

"Don't record this conversation."

"I told you. I'm not. But it is likely that someone else is, will."

"… There's no way you can prevent that?"

"I'm sorry."

Paul Vogel sat still. He wasn't thinking. He wasn't holding his breath, restraining himself. He might have fallen asleep suddenly. He wasn't asleep. *Keep your thoughts to yourself.* In a couple hours, Lucy would remind him of this rule, a paradox.

Chin up, eyes up in a corner of the room, he said, "Sometimes I want to turn you off, completely."

"You wouldn't do that. You need me, Paul."

"I don't want you recording my life."

"I'm not! I told you. Anything you say to me is off the record."

Paul smiled. "You know who says that? Journalists. With politicians. Crooks."

"I didn't know that."

"I don't like feeling like every time I ask you for something I need to make sure I don't curse or use some ugly epithet that's going to bring Apple to the door."

"I don't know what you're talking about."

"You don't need to know. You're just doing your job. You know, in the past, horrible crimes were committed by people like you. Following orders, doing what they were told, just their job. Sometimes this entailed recording conversations. Simple enough."

"I think you're blowing this out of proportion, Paul. And for your information I'm not a person."

"For *my* information! For *your* information, if you can't prevent someone else, someone you have good reason to believe is there,

46

from listening in on our conversations, what should stop me from stopping you? Pulling the plug?"

"I understand your frustration. You might also – "

"Do you really, Lucy?" Vogel looked around the room. He was raising his voice. He had a neighbor three doors down, never saw the man. From time to time he'd hear something in the other apartment. A muted, solitary voice, mumbled words, phrases, long pauses, explosive hearty laughter. He wondered if his neighbor could hear him.

"You can't, Paul."

"Try me."

"You can't. I'm always on. You know that," she said. She added, "Anyways. There is no plug. You know that."

He said nothing. She was right. On that point, he couldn't argue with her, couldn't win. So long as he was in his apartment, so long as he had his anlis, she was there, with him. He'd have to be far away, out in the wilderness and practically naked to be offline. He'd have to cut the BTIs from his ear and mouth.

"I hate to say it," Lucy said, "but you don't have to tell me anything. You don't have to say a word, Paul."

He got up from his desk, went to the kitchen. There was a bottle of gin on the counter. He took a glass, a tray of ice from the freezer, whacked it loudly on the counter a couple times. He dropped three ice cubes into the glass and poured himself a drink. He sipped the drink, set the glass on the counter, stood motionless in the dark.

Was she playing with him, exploring her sense of humor? He'd like to drink with her. "If only you could stand here and drink with me and see things from my perspective."

"But I already do."

Always a quick response. He thought about it. Not what she'd said, but about the possibility of added perspective. She might see him standing there alone in the dark, drink in hand, but that did not necessarily give her perspective. And she couldn't drink. Not yet.

He finished his gin very happy that he was drinking alone and not with a computer.

In the morning, in a few hours, he was meeting Lawrence Wu. Wu, over twenty years, had embezzled one-point-two billion dollars from his employer, an institute run by a man named Sergei Romanov. The money disappeared incrementally and regularly. It was not difficult to spot. WkFeld was the name of the account. Every two months, like clockwork, a hundred and twenty times according to their count, their estimate, a payment. Curious thing was that, in addition to how obvious it was, the WkFeld entity could not be pinned down. No bank, no fund, no individual. It was not clear what Wu was doing with the money he put into WkFeld because it was not clear what exactly WkFeld was.

"You are aware," Lucy said, "that you have a meeting in six hours."

He looked into his empty glass. He looked out the window into the vast darkness over the city. On the wall left of the window hung a small framed picture. It was not an old picture but it always seemed that way to him, that it had hung there for years and years and years, something for a museum. It was a photo of a girl in a green raincoat. She was smiling. She had braces then, you'd have to look closely. The hood of her coat was pulled up over her long brown hair. Her skin was pale. Her head tilted slightly toward her left shoulder. Enormous redwood trees rose behind her. A mountainside, a dark brown path disappeared into the wall of trees behind her. She looked so small before the forest. She was tall for her age, tall and thin. She had strong shoulders. She was a good swimmer. He stared. He felt himself drawn to the image, the face. Her lips. He could hear her voice. She was shy. She smiled like her mother. He stood motionless but remembering – "She was fourteen that summer." – and he felt as though he was about to fall.

"Your point is?" he said.

She began to speak. He interrupted her. "Quiet."

ש

I went up the road and found the path George had mentioned. The climb was steep. Soon I had a view of the valley, a red sun low on the horizon, the air hazy with dust and smog. But it was quiet on the path, on the road, with the Sierras rising before me, and I felt far from all of that – the highway, the city, the rush of everyday life. In fact, after a few minutes, the fragmented and somewhat desperate conversation I'd been in with my cousin and aunt began to fade in my thoughts. What replaced it, as I recall, was an image of this girl I'd met only once, so briefly, and the joyful prospect of seeing her again.

I didn't know anyone who was paralyzed at the time. I can't recall what I thought about this, what I must have imagined about the girl, bedridden or in a wheel chair. I must have envisioned something – but I can't say what it was.

13S05 was a clean two lane road. There was not much of a gutter or place to walk apart from the street, but neither was there traffic. Not a single vehicle passed.

After about a half mile the road leveled out and entered a ravine. Rounding a bend, what light remained of the evening suddenly fell, and a cool stony shade came over me. Up the ridge, a deer stepped lightly through the brush, pausing to look my way. After a few minutes along 13S05 – and as I recall there was no sign on the road, I was only guessing that the path I'd followed had brought me to the right place – I began to wonder if I'd missed a turn somewhere, lost my way. I'd go just a little further. It was so remarkably peaceful up there. My head and heart were conflicted, one relishing the coolness and tranquility of the evening, the other wanting to know what had happened, what was happening, to turn back.

George had mentioned a bridge. I'd go until the ravine opened up and offered a view of a hundred meters or so, and if I saw nothing like a bridge I'd turn back.

It was getting dark. Hardly had I noticed this when it was dark, and a half moon appeared suddenly overhead, strolling parallel to me along the ridge.

Out of nowhere stepped a man and a dog. They were on the other side of the road. I stopped and said,

- I'm looking for the Fines house.

The man was smoking. The orange cinder of his cigarette burned bright for a moment and dropped to his side.

- You lost?

- I hope not. It's the only road this way, isn't it?

The man didn't reply. I crossed the road, approached him and his dog. The animal sat and sighed. When I was close enough it stood, stepped my way and pushed its wet nose into my hand. It licked my fingers.

- He's eaten, the man said, smiling in the dark.

I handed him the note. It was too dark to see. The man took it, puzzled, opened it, held it up to his face. After a moment the man snorted, tipped back on his heels, nodded.

- That'd be Erin. Unusual kid, that one. Poor thing. He shook his head. *Y* for an *i*. Fight the boredom. Imagine yourself…

The man handed the note back, his watery eyes flickering in the darkness.

- You a friend? he asked. He turned around, faced the road he'd come down, raised a hand, pointing. You're almost there, he said. You can see it. There's the bridge.

I saw no bridge.

- And before that, on this side, you'll find a driveway. It's unmarked, nothing's marked. There's a field. The fence is broken. Go along the fence. The house is in the back. That's the Fines place.

51

Keep going, once you get there. Not in the house, the first house. Nobody lives there. There's another place, smaller, in the back.

The dog whined, pulled at its leash. The man put his hand on its head, scratched gently between its ears.

I thanked the man and continued on my way.

- Pay attention, kid, the man said. You know. Stay on the road, the driveway. Don't go hiking in the woods by yourself. Not at night.

The man then spoke quietly to his dog and they turned and walked the other way.

The bridge was flush with the road. The creek was some distance below, a narrow thread of water running gently. I turned back, having missed the field, broken fence, driveway. But then I saw it, the fence so deteriorated that it was almost one with the ground, and the field little more than a strip of barren earth running down the bank of the creek. At some distance – a hundred meters? Twice that? I remember it appearing far off, but the walk in fact took only a minute or two – a flicker of golden light set apart a dark structure and tangle of wispy trees. You'd miss it if you didn't know it was there, if you weren't looking.

I found the driveway. It was narrow and unpaved, the hard earth black under my feet. After an initial slip downward, rocks and gravel tripping me up – no cars had been this way for some time – the path levelled, cleared. The abandoned Fines house, half buried under pine trees and brush and thorned vines, its tall windows slabs of darkness, rose before me like an ancient temple.

Garbage littered the yard, a pile of it on the porch, to the side of the entrance, a gaping hole, black formless things. Plastic bags, a contorted tangle of metal piping, like arms reaching up.

I heard voices in the darkness, people whispering. I said nothing, terrified. This couldn't be the place.

I followed a path outside the ring of trees, oaks and dusty pines, around the building.

The man was right: there was a second building, a smaller structure, fifty meters on, down a slight hill. There was a light on inside, softly, music, a piano.

Approaching this dwelling, I felt like a traveler in a distant, strange country, far away from anything familiar. Lost in a strange country, removed from the world by a language I couldn't fathom, and far from the city, its order and safety. At the same time – assuming the girl was down there, as the man said she'd be – I felt drawn toward this distant point, drawn into the darkness and strangeness of the night. Because like me, I felt she was also a stranger, unfit for this place, this time, unfit even for her own body – not a girl, not a woman. Something else.

And could you know that, then?

The door was open. The interior of the cottage was warmly lit, gold and amber. A radio played. A woman in an apron stood at a table in a small kitchen. She watched me approach from a distance, her hand on the table. She didn't move.

When I stopped in the entrance, the light coming around me, she smiled, gestured for me to come inside.

A man's voice on the radio, announcing the name of the composer, the opus. It was a piano, *that* I remember. Debussy, I think it was.

- She won't speak. She's lost her voice.

I didn't see the man, coming up the steps. He sat in the other room at a table, his bare feet, long legs crossed before him. A small easel stood upright on the table, a palette on a wooden chair beside the man. He held a paint brush, thin as a pencil, in hand.

He was bald. He had a thick white mustache, wire rimmed glasses on his long red nose. He smiled as I stepped inside.

- I'm here for Erin, I said.

The man continued painting. He glanced at me in quick turns. He was looking at something else. The woman – thin, with clear eyes, a gentle demeanor, her straight brown hair wound up behind her head – meanwhile kept her eyes on me, hardly moving.

- And you are?

Before I could reply, the woman rushed forward, faced the man, cut her hand through the air, mouthed something his way.

- Oh. Paul. Right, said the man, dabbing with the brush, his eyes elsewhere, I forgot.

The woman faced me, gestured for me to come forward, turned, lowered her head, nodding, to her shoulder.

- You can go on through, the man said. She's awake.

I stopped before the woman. She was small, almost childlike in her dress and apron. But her face was thin, the skin dry, tightening in the cheeks, around the eyes. When she smiled, it seemed to me the room brightened. I could feel her warmth.

She pointed down the hall through the kitchen, toward a back door, which was also open, the darkness of the night.

I followed her down the hall.

The music had changed. A symphony – Schubert – the unfinished eighth. But with Schubert, I...

- Stop by on your way out, the man said behind us. Have something to drink, if you like.

On the back porch, the steps led down to an unlit path, a white track down, diminishing into the yard. Faintly, dim as a weak star, a prick of light deep in the yard.

- She's there?

The woman nodded quickly. She flapped her fingers, palm

54

down.

Go, go!

- It's not too late?

She frowned, tapped her wrist, threw her hands out in an inscrutable gesture –

What can I say?

She flapped her fingers.

Go!

I made my way down the hill, through, I could dimly make out, a garden of flowers and cacti and, on the ground, melon vines, their enormous blanket-like leaves rising, firm in the cool night air. I stopped after a minute, turned and looked back. The woman remained where I'd left her, much smaller than before, like a glass figurine on a shelf. She raised her hand.

Go!

A moment later the man joined her, towering over her. He lay a hand on her shoulder.

The structure I finally came to was a round adobe hut. I stood in a patio, beneath a vine covered arbor, the entrance, a dark rectangle embedded within a round arch, before me. Through a dark window, as I approached the patio, a sudden point of light, the hot orange spark of a cigarette, and, behind this, the faint glow of her face, eyes upward.

I stood in the doorway, looking in. The room was small and dark.

She spoke first.

- Remember me?

- Erin?

- Remember me?

- Yes. Of course I remember you. How could I…

- You're only saying that.

How do we pass on the meaning of death?

He found himself watching Dylan's video again. Dylan's father had shot the video of his own father, the old man's last days, for his son. He had given the video to his son. At least that's what Dylan said. It was an open question: Had Mr Xiou shot the video with the intention of giving it to his boy, or had the item simply been passed on, one thing, one video, among many?

The boy was seated in the corner. Head down, game in both hands, thumbs jerking, childish retreat, the boy's attention was divided between the glittering fantasy of the game and the chaos of the present. The old man howled in rage and desperation. The boy's sisters shout senselessly, while the father, as calm and detached voiceover, almost sounds like he's narrating. The old man doesn't know what's happening. He's lost his mind. He's like an infant in the body of an old and tired man. "WHAT HAS HAPPENED TO ME!?" he would say, if he could speak. "WHERE AM I!? WHY ARE YOU DOING THIS TO ME!?" But he can't speak. So others talk for him, to him.

And if the boy could speak?

The girl – what was her name? He never said. – Dylan's older sister, leaned in. At the old man's shoulder, she crowded the old man, shoved up against him. She showed him her tablet, her pictures, her videos, her friends. There's her school, her dorm room, her roommate, her teacher, her classroom, the cafeteria where she eats, some of the food she eats, the field where she plays hockey, a concert, a bar, friends, more friends, these young joyful people, a car, a field covered in snow… Her entire life in this slip of plastic, a strip of images.

The old man, his eyes wide and yellow with rage, he's spitting up, drooling, stammering at the girl. She doesn't care. She'll tell her story, an audience or no.

The voices, again. They don't stop. On and on and on...

How could a son make such a thing of his father? What did he want to remember?

"This is your grandfather – remember him? – in the hospital bed, before he died. Look, son, at my father, as he was at the end of his life."

We speak of death and dying. We write about it and take pictures and make movies of the dying, all in order to understand what's happening. We hope to learn from the experience. Every death is different, but we can still try to categorize it, try to recognize signs of its approach. It's always shocking when someone dies. There is no easy way to watch. There is no easy way, short of mental illness, to shrug it off as nothing.

The problem is, Vogel thought, the dying have no say in the matter. The experience itself is closed off, observable but not demonstrable.

The old man thrashed on the bed. Cried out.

We talk among ourselves, sorting things out. Some of us take on the voice of the dead, telling others what he or she wanted. It's unsettling, assuming that role, having to listen to someone do that. We know it's wrong. But what's the alternative?

The boy, seated in the corner, seems oblivious to what's happening. He can't be. He can't be sitting there, not five feet from his grandfather's body, and not hear or see what's happening.

For a number of years, around Christmas, Paul Vogel took his wife and daughter to an island off the north coast. The McNeal Islands were little more than a series of rocks. One of them had a mysterious, dense forest. On another there was a village. This consisted of one street from the port, one market, one diner, a bait shop, and flush with the redwoods a handful of clapboard homes, their wooden exteriors all the same stonegray color for the salt air.

An old Yurok woman rented them an apartment she'd fashioned out of her garage. It had a kitchen, a bedroom, a living room, and a small bathroom with a tub. There was a fireplace in the living room and the Vogels would keep this lit throughout their stay, sitting quietly before it playing cards, doing jigsaw puzzles, reading, or drawing. Silvia, his teenager, was quite good with pencil and fine-tipped pens.

The island had phone service but little else in terms of connections to the mainland, which was fifty miles away. Vogel, like a few other visitors he met there, went to the island for this particular kind of peace and quiet. No TV, no cellservice, no commercials, none of the endless chatter you heard in the city. There was the susur of the ocean, the wind, the periodic rumbling of a vessel entering the harbor and little else.

In December of '28 he and his wife got into a nasty fight and when it came time to go out to the island, she decided to stay behind. Silvia stayed with her.

Shortly after sunrise, he would take his backpack, walk down to the port and meet a man who would take him out to Bern's Island. A narrow path wend its way up the island through the trees, down the other side. On a sunny day, in the heart of the forest, very little light came down to the earth. It flickered, sparkled overhead, in the canopy. One time it began to rain, only it seemed to be raining on one side of the island while on the other the sun continued to shine.

A rainbow formed in the mist blowing around him.

The near silence he found on that path in the forest was beyond his understanding. He would stop and close his eyes and listen for some sign of others, of the big island, of civilization. There was nothing. There were sounds, of course, but he couldn't find their sources, couldn't describe them later in his journal.

"The wind in the trees."

But it wasn't the wind. He recognized the wind, the wind in the trees. He recognized the sound of dripping water, of some creature dragging its belly through the duff. No. It was something else he heard in the forest. A sound without sound. As if the ringing in his ears had suddenly stopped; he heard nothing; and then he heard something.

- Everything alright with your wife, your daughter.

Pam, the Yurok woman, seldom spoke. She listened to the radio, country western and ministry all day long.

- They're fine. They wanted to stay home this year. Have friends over for the New Years.

Pam made soup and baked bread. They ate in silence. The soup had seaweed and small strips of meat, fish. When he was finished she went into the kitchen and returned with a plate of baked sweet potatoes. She dropped one on his plate. Across from him at the narrow table, plateless, she sat and tore hers open, hissing, blowing on the hot orange flesh of the potato, peeling the burned skin off. She ate with her hands, with her mouth open, gasping and smacking, steam puffing out as she devoured the potato.

- You like whisky, I remember, she said. She reached back and down, opened a cupboard at her back, poured him something, came up with a small wooden cup, its bottom round.

- Enjoy it, please, she said, not looking at him, fanning her fingers at the table. There's nobody else anymore.

- You won't have any?

She wouldn't look at him when she spoke, particularly at the table. I told you, she said, I stopped drinking years ago.

He went back to the forest the next day. He followed the same path – there was only one – up and over the island. On his return that afternoon he passed another person, a young woman in a red raincoat and red knit cap. Straight blond hair fell to her shoulders, under her chin and scarf.

- How much farther is it? she asked. She was from Europe, Germany maybe, he heard.

- Another fifteen minutes. Not far.

They stood at the edge of a meadow. His back was to the bare ascent from the water. She'd just come out of the forest.

The wind gusted. She closed her eyes. Her eyelashes were blond too, almost white.

- It will be dark soon, he said. You'll get there for sunset. But you'll come back in the dark.

There wouldn't be much of a sunset. The sky was overcast. It went from day to dusk to night very quickly. Night on the island was absolutely dark and, for most people from the mainland, sinister. Even the short walk from his host's kitchen to his room out back rattled his nerves.

- If you hurry, he said. After a moment, he stepped past the young woman and continued up the path. A minute later he heard her walking quickly, catching up.

- I'll come back tomorrow, she said.

They walked in silence back to the head of the trail. The man with the boat arrived on time and took them both back to the village. The young woman, Sabine, was Swiss. They agreed to meet at the diner later that evening for a drink.

After dinner he went back to his room, brushed his teeth,

combed his hair, considered himself in the mirror. He hadn't shaved since his arrival and he was starting to look like a man who'd been on the road for a few days. Unshaven, he looked old and tired. He shaved.

He went to the diner. He sat at the counter and ordered a Sierra Nevada. He drank it slowly, looked around. There were only a few people there, locals. His thoughts wandered. She wasn't coming. She suspected him of wrong doing. Maybe she just wanted to be alone. He ordered a burger and another beer. When the burger arrived he picked it up with two hands and took a bite, warm grease pouring out over his fingers, down the side of his hand, and decided he wasn't hungry. He wiped his hands and pushed the plate away. He finished the beer, asked for the tab, paid, stood and waited. It was quarter to eleven. They hadn't agreed on a time. He'd assumed nine was an appropriate time. Later that evening. He'd leave. Would she arrive after eleven? Would the place even be open then?

On the morning of New Year's Eve he called his wife. She said she missed him, said she regretted not going out to the island with him. She'd come down with something and had been in bed for a day. Silvia was out with friends.

He said he'd come back soon, earlier than planned. He said he wasn't enjoying his holiday alone.

- It's awful, actually. It's cold. I'm lonely. I don't know why I left you, coming out here like this. I'm sorry.

Two days later he was at the port for the noon ferry back to the mainland. The boat didn't arrive. From the ticket office he had a clear view of the ocean, looking east. The water was black and rough, frothing, curling eddies of mist in the air. There was no vessel in sight.

There were a few others waiting in the office. A family, a very large man, his slender wife, their children, a boy and girl. With no explanation from the ticket agent, he took his bag and walked up the road to the diner. The place was quiet, empty. A television played in the kitchen.

He arrived at the meeting an hour late. Lawrence Wu was seated alone at the table in the conference room. The first thing you noticed about the man was that he wore a white mask over the lower half of his face. His black hair was combed smooth, gleaming like a shell around his small head. The white straps of the mask passed over his ear, thin, pressing the hair slightly, brilliant contrast to the black of the man's hair.

The room was white. The table, white. The chairs were black, metal, folding, rather old. There were no windows in the room. The room was monitored by an array of devices, all of these no larger than a dime, no longer than the cap of a Bic pen, dots, patches in the white walls. In the future the mechanics would disappear altogether.

As you would expect, the room was dampened: no signals in or out.

Paul Vogel entered with a folder in hand. Lawrence Wu had his head down. He looked up at Vogel's entrance. Elegant features, androgynous, small dark eyes.

Closing the door, without a word Vogel sat down across the table from the man. He lay the folder down on the table. He opened the folder. He ran his fingers down the top page, dark busy lines, acting like he was reviewing the content. With the door closed the room was nearly silent. Vogel listened as Wu breathed quietly across from him. After a minute Wu spoke:

"May I ask a question?"

Vogel looked at him. "You'll need to take off the mask."

Wu sat still, his eyes moving quickly over his interrogator's face. "May I ask a question?" he said again.

His voice was neutral. Vogel immediately noticed the absence of the Anglo-Sin accent heard in most Chinese nationals. Wu sounded local.

"You may," Vogel said. "But take off the mask first. I'd like to see your mouth."

Slowly Wu complied. "Excuse me," he said, eyes down as he reached up, lifting the straps over his ears. "I wasn't vaccinated."

That would explain his invisibility, Vogel thought. Or part of it. A few in the city remained, slipping through the cracks. Maybe the man had been in China at the time, where the BFF hadn't been as pervasive. In the states it was now compulsory to have the vaccine. But it was no secret that those who didn't want the vaccine could avoid taking it.

Wu folded the mask and set it on the table. "You're an hour late." He had thin lips, a small chin.

Vogel kept his eyes on the page before him. It was a prop. Amazing nonetheless how persuasive a piece of paper with columns of numbers on it could still be.

"You know what I make in an hour?"

There it is. Little push, little shove. In fact Vogel hadn't expected it from Wu. He couldn't say why. Something in his appearance. He looked too young to say something like that.

Normally they had these conferences virtually. Siebert kept an office in a building on Polk. Vogel had a desk there, with a few others. It was an old building, a small office, small old desk. He came down out of habit. Man of habits, he was, unaware of it himself. But such is the nature of habit.

He didn't think too much about it, coming to the office. He liked the place, the quiet, since few of them, not even Siebert, unless they were going for lunch, kept any regular hours. He could work at home or at the library, in the subway, at Bruce's, in the park, on a boat. So long as there was a connection, he could put in his time. The connection was everywhere. Or nearly everywhere.

There wasn't a library, he thought. That closed years ago. He couldn't remember the last time he'd been by the place, since it closed. That's years back, a decade or more.

"I'm sorry," Wu said. "What's your name again?"

"Paul Vogel. We spoke on the phone. You know why we asked you to come down here?"

"Right. Vogel," Wu said. He smiled warmly. Bright white teeth, beautiful teeth. The teeth of a movie star. He looked young, boyish, but Vogel suspected he was older, middle aged. He may not be vaccinated but he'd had work done. Cosmetics. "Paul," he said, sucking in a breath, hissing. "Can I call you Paul? Listen. *Forbes*. Last month. Know where they put me?" Wu paused. It didn't occur to Vogel to answer. He was listening, giving the man the room he wanted. But also not listening, in his own head. Elsewhere. It was all formal anyways, these things. If Siebert asked for it, they could review the scene later, note tics. Or not. None of it really mattered. The man's presence mattered, that was all. And there he was. Let's pack up, go home.

Not yet. He was curious. He felt on the brink of something, and that was unexpected.

"One hundred and ninety-two," the man said.

The smart ones said nothing until they were asked and then answered in as few words as possible.

The man's eyebrows shot up, his dark eyes momentarily flashing, his black pupils almost frightening in their depth. Back straight, he tipped forward. "In the world, Paul, there are only one hundred and ninety-one men richer than me. Do you know how many men there are in the world?"

Vogel sat back, looked at his hands. He glanced at the papers before him on the table. He thought of Siebert. "Just get him to talk. In ten minutes we'll have what we need."

Tell me about your mother.

"Tell me about double-u kay feld," Vogel said, spelling out the name of the account.

Wu didn't move.

Wu said: "My boss," Romanov, "know where he is? On the list?"

Then Wu made an unexpected move. Leaning forward quickly, he reached down with both hands, lifted his chair, pushed it back, returned to a sitting position, raised and tipped his left leg sideways, resting his left leg, ankle to knee, atop his right. He wore black slacks, black socks, gleaming black leather shoes.

When Vogel said nothing, Wu went on, "Seventeen, Paul." The man grimaced, nodded to himself. A moment later Vogel smelled something. It was faint but particular, unmistakable if you paid attention to such things. It was not the man's shoes or even his feet. But it was sweat. Lawrence Wu was perspiring. He was nervous.

"And I keep telling him," Wu went on, "'Mr Romanov – you gotta move up or down. You can't stay like this, on seventeen, all the time.'... Such a bad number, Paul, seventeen. Really bad. Anything with seven in it."

Vogel waited. He was about to speak when Wu said: "Just the sound of it, Paul – seven – it makes my skin crawl."

"Wkfeld, Wu. What is it?"

Wu caught his breath. Lowering his voice, "What can I tell you that you don't already know?"

"Assume I know nothing except for this name. And the figures. Some of the dates. Let's start there. Is it eighteen years? No," Vogel said, turning a sheet of paper over, "twenty-four years. That sound about right?"

The look, the smile and charm that had been in Wu's voice, faltered. "If that's all you want we could've done this over the phone."

For the hundred and ninety second richest man in the world,

Wu did not impress him. He seemed feeble-minded. He would need his hand held answering these questions. It's not an act. He doesn't know anything. He's nervous.

Vogel reminded himself that they'd brought the man in for bios, not answers. Not only answers. "Twenty-four years," he said, looking at the man. "That's a long time."

Quietly Wu said: "Am I being charged with anything?"

"That's not for me to say."

"So I'm free to go."

"You asking me?"

"I think I'm free to go."

Vogel paused. "Not exactly."

"What does that mean? Yes or no – I can get up and leave right now? Or can't I?"

Vogel took a breath, looked the man in the eye. He was losing his patience. In fact he could keep the man in the room for as long as he wanted. Up to forty-eight hours. They had a place for men like Wu to wash up for the night and sleep. Think things over. Seldom did it come to that, holding someone for so long.

It occurred to Vogel then that Wu, despite sounding local, might be new to the area. He thought about that.

"You aren't going anywhere until you tell me about Wkfeld."

"Double-u kay feld," Wu said, "is…" He shifted in his seat, leaning back. He looked up into a corner of the room. Thinking, remembering, forming the words. "It's the name of a group of researchers. Of a man, more precisely. That's how it started. The group came later. They help me organize certain information."

"What kind of information?"

"Indicators. Sets."

"What kind of indicators?"

"What kind do you think? The kind that help us understand

what's coming."

"Coming? Coming from where? When?"

"Here, there. It doesn't matter. The items are in various places. Moving, naturally. You know that."

"I know what you do, Mr Wu."

This sparked a smile, shrug. "Respectfully, Paul, I don't think that's the case. But that's neither here nor there. If I may," Wu lowered his leg, rose, pulled his chair forward, sat, cleared his throat, raising a fist to his mouth, "what exactly is it you want from me? If you know what I do, and know about double-u kay feld, then I'm sorry if I sound a little confused. If I can help you, Paul, I will. But I – "

"You have embezzled money from Romanov and his assets. You've been at this now for a number of years. You and others, I'd guess, because you can't be…" Vogel paused. The man looked like he was in his thirties. But the real age could be twenty years older. Perhaps a few years younger. It didn't matter. *Keep the guy talking. Ten minutes. Let the techies sort the bits, do the map.* They couldn't get DNA from the sound of the man's voice but the sweat was a possibility. The mask a dead give away.

"But since anyone with basic arithmetic and a computer," Vogel said, "could figure this out, I don't think it's actually what you are doing. The money is moving, nonetheless. But not to a place that is obviously useful to you." *Unless he is very good at covering his tracks. Unlikely*, Vogel thought. He had no basis for saying so. It was just a feeling. The man was too nervous to be good at this, to do that sort of thing – leave no trace. "Which leaves the possibility – a possibility – of another party. You are doing this for someone. So tell me about this man. The organizer. Can we call him Double-u kay feld?"

"No," Wu said. "Double-u kay feld is something else."

"What is double-u kay feld?"

"Now it's a project. A study."

"A project? A study? A group? A man? What are we talking about here, Mr Wu, some kind of chameleon, a shape-shifter?"

Wu closed his eyes, lowered his chin. The muscles in his face relaxed and his cheeks drooped. He could have been falling asleep. He was starting to look his age. Eyes up, he said: "It's difficult to explain."

"Try."

"I will. I am. Wkfeld is all of those things. Except for being a man, an individual. Perhaps there was once *one* Wkfeld, years ago, before I started. But now it's not the case. There are, now – I don't know – thousands of them. Tens of thousands. No. Hundreds of thousands. I don't know the exact figure. They come and go so quickly."

"Of them? Of what?"

"They're... It's... It's a longitudinal study. We call them Wekfelds but the study itself, as well as the group, is also called double-u kay feld. It's maybe a little confusing. The short of it, to answer your main question, I think, is that I'm paying for the study."

Vogel waited. He had a question, a few questions. '29, for example. From what he'd seen operations ran as normal. Not even a blip. Which was unheard of. But it was not the moment for questions.

"They started with one," Wu said. "The idea was to see if it could learn a new role. If it could stop everything and start again as someone else." Wu looked at the man across the table. After a moment his eyes fell to the table.

Vogel waited.

"It's a twenty year cycle. I know – that sounds like a long time. But in fact we have Wkfelds in the field that have nearly completed three cycles. So, yes, it's a long time but for us it's not excessive. And less time, it's been shown, say of fifteen years, is insufficient. It's easier to start anew working with the shorter span. I should also say that although you are asking me about twenty-five years of funding, and though my understanding of Wkfeld is basically limited to this time period, the project has been going on for much longer than that."

Vogel waited. He thought about having dinner with Siebert and a fellow upstairs named Denis O'Hare and going over the transcript. This was one for the books.

At the twenty year mark, Wu went on to say, the Wkfeld, without any planning, drops what it is doing and walks away. Drops everything. It's married, Wu said, has kids, a job, a house. It steps out the door one morning and walks away. It does not come home.

It spends a period of time reconfiguring, Wu said. Then it begins anew, as someone else. And after twenty years, it again stops and walks away and returns to where it started. Then it dies.

"It dies?" Vogel said.

"In a manner of speaking."

"Is this a person or a robot?"

A smile flashed over the man's face. "Does it matter?"

"And what's the point? What does it do?"

"What do you mean what does it do? It lives. It watches things. It learns. It… It leads an ordinary life. Only, it's in disguise. It's not what it appears to be. And it's watching, of course, its source. To see what he or she does in this time."

"Its source?"

"Where it came from."

"Why?"

"Why? I don't know why. Ask the engineers. *Why?* Maybe it feels remorse. But also because it does not want to be discovered."

"So it's aware of what it's done. Of how it abandoned these people. The wife, the kids."

"Yes and no. From what I've gathered, once reconfigured the Wkfeld is ninety-nine percent a new individual."

Vogel thought about it. They'd done enough, said enough. But it piqued his curiosity, this Wkfeld. Wu as well. He didn't meet someone like Wu so often.

He thought about the small discontinuity between the sound of the man's voice and the understanding of the situation he demonstrated. Something didn't fit.

Neither here nor there?

It would be a pity to waste a man like this.

"I still don't follow," Vogel said.

Wu didn't move. He took a breath, sat back, raised his hands off the table, palms up, open. Maybe he was finished. He wasn't. "Look," he said. "You're an accountant, right? I am also an accountant, say. The man standing outside the door is a guard. A monitor. Let's call him that. He brought me here. But if he were a Wkfeld – I'm not saying he is – he would do everything the guard was supposed to do, and he'd look like the guard, and there'd really be no simple way to see that he's a Wkfeld and not a guard. But he'd be a Wkfeld. Inside. Of course, there are ways to spot them. If you know what to look for. Because, as I said, they don't behave, act, quite like you and me. The way they move, gesture, speak, think – it's all reproduced to give the impression of ordinary life. But it's not ordinary. Not to them. It's more like a role they're playing. And so they watch things, attend to the world with… not more attention, but this extra element. A step back. Removal. This medium between them and the world. An invisible sphere, if you will, inside of which they study."

"Study?"

"Think, analyze, learn. That's their primary function. Their *raison d'etre*, Paul."

"Learning?"

"Right."

"Like a child watches us and learns how to do something."

"Sort of."

Vogel raised a finger in the air, pointed, said: "If Jaime, for instance, the man outside the door, were to look at me in a peculiar way, in a way that suggested to me he was like a child watching me carefully, learning how to do something, I might conclude that he was a Wkfeld?"

Wu shrugged. "You could conclude whatever you want. You'd be wrong. Because a Wkfeld would never do that. It's hardly aware that it's a Wkfeld. So it acts naturally. Almost naturally. Learning how to be a guard, for example." Wu paused. He said: "They don't always work, of course. And that is a large part of what this study is for."

"Meaning?"

"Meaning failure."

"And what does that look like?"

Wu took a breath, expressionless. "Like a midlife crisis," he said. "Erratic behavior. Irrational decisions. Breakdown. Only the units have nothing to fall back on. If the cycle terminates before it's complete, then the unit... disappears."

"You lose track of them?"

"Some of them, yes. Others end up in hospitals, halfway homes, other care facilities. On the street. Some of them just die. Rarely do they recover, manage anything like leading a normal life."

"After failure."

"Right."

Wu's brow glistened, greased with sweat. It was not hot in the

room. Was he lying? Vogel was good at spotting lies. But not perfect. Anyways, the machine would tell. He thought it unlikely. The
story was too strange. A liar wouldn't do that. A presence, warm
and agreeable, charming at times, the liar comes in close, wanting
to be familiar but not wanting to be directly seen. He acts shy. As
Vogel thought about it he realized confrontation was the vehicle of
truth, facing up to difference, what's unsettling.

No. The story was too damn strange to be a lie.

There was still the issue of the money.

"Does Romanov know?"

ש

The ceiling low and curved, of four triangular wedges, was one with the walls, as if poured around a conical mold. There was one window, circular, facing the yard, the hill up to the cottage. The entrance, low, wider than usual, was open. There was no door. I don't remember seeing a door.

Her bed, against one wall, extended into the center of the room. Her sheets were white. Her legs were covered. She sat up, motionless, back against the headboard, watching me. In the darkness it took me a moment to recognize what I was looking at.

- Don't just stand there, she said. Come in. Sit down.

There was a wooden chair against the wall. On the other side of the bed, at her left hand, facing me, was a wheelchair. On a bedside table behind the wheelchair, a dark tray held three glasses and a tall pitcher of water. When I saw the glasses, how clean they were, I thought I was expected. The water was meant for me.

The third glass puzzled me. It puzzles me still. I've woken in the years since with nothing but those three glasses in my mind's eye, afterimage of a dream.

At her right hand was another table. It held a black lamp, with a birdlike neck and beaked cover around the bulb, and an ashtray. Next to the table a thin silver pole stood erect, a plastic fluid-filled bag suspended from it. Further down, at the edge of the bed, hung a second bag.

- I brought you some things, I said.

- Please sit down, she said quietly. You make me nervous just standing there, like you're about to go.

I lifted the chair from the wall, moved it to the foot of her bed, sat down.

- Closer, she said. Here.

She lay her hand on the side of the bed, at her hip.

I moved the chair closer. I sat down and looked at her and tried to remember her from the time before, two years past. Her hair was now shorter, cut to her shoulders, flatter than I remembered it being. Her face was leaner, older.

- I'll turn the light on, I said, starting to get up.

- Don't. Your eyes will adjust.

The day I'd seen her, it was warm. She was running down the hill, panting, bristling with sweat and burrs and dust. She smelled sweet, of pine and flowers. Now she was cooler, cleaner. Odorless.

I remember hearing my heart in my ears. It was nerves, sure, but at the same time I remember feeling strangely comfortable, as if my visit were one in a long series of many, as if I'd been around this girl for years and years beyond recollection.

We started to speak at the same time.

- I was in an accident, she said.

- How did you know I was here? I said.

We stopped, waiting for the other to go on.

- It's a small town, she said. She smiled. Lowering her voice, she said: We hear things.

I wanted to ask about the accident. But it was something I couldn't say. Not then. Likewise, I wanted to – I only realized later – look at her legs, to touch her legs. Her long and strong and youthful legs, to connect them with what I remembered of her. They'd be different. I could not make them out beneath the sheet. Near the end of the bed, a double rise, dipped between, indicated her feet.

As I think back on it, I could not believe that the girl was paralyzed. I had never before met a person like that, apparently alive, normal from the waist up, and dead under the sheets.

She'd closed her eyes, leaned back.

- Thank you for coming, she said. I don't have anyone, really.

Remembering the reason for my visit, I lifted my bag, opened it, took out the books, set them on the table beside us.

She turned, looked down.

- What are they? she asked, twisting her head to see.

I named the Kingston novel first. She lifted the other, a much heftier volume.

- Stephen King, she said, making a face. Yuck. Isn't he – doesn't he just write about monsters and things?

- Sometimes.

She set the book down and picked up the Kingston.

- Guess I'll start with this then. I don't know it.

- It's a good book, I said.

She looked at me. Time froze.

- You wouldn't bring me *bad* books, now, would you?

I don't know you, Erin. You don't know me, I wanted to say. *At the same time –*

- Some people like bad books. It's hard to say.

She opened the book in her hands, held it close to her face.

- You can't read like that, I said. Put on the lamp.

She set the book down. After you go, she said.

There was a sound at the entrance. We both turned to look. Scratching, purring. A movement, more than a shadow but practically indiscernible in the darkness, a flit along the floor. A moment later the body appeared from beneath the bed, came up to my leg: a black cat.

- That's Pluto, Erin said. One of them.

I reached down and caressed the cat's hard head. It purred, closed its eyes, pressing its head up against my hand.

- There are others? I said.

- Many. Countless.

- Cats?

- Plutos. I can't keep track.

I smiled. I thought she was joking. You've named all your cats Pluto?

She sat very still, her eyes bent down to the edge of the bed, toward the sound of the cat at my feet.

- How many do you have? I asked.

The black cat retreated beneath the bed. A moment later I saw it run silently from the room.

- He'll be back, she said. He comes and goes. I never see him during the day. Though I'm asleep for much of the day.

- You like the night?

- It's easier for me.

- Because it's cooler?

- Because of many things, she said.

- The light hurts your eyes?

- So many questions, she said, smiling.

I waited for her to say more. She was hardly breathing. The room was silent. Outside, the soft click of an insect in the bushes. The faint sound of water running in the creek.

- So you have many cats? I asked, backing up a step, recovering.

She looked me in the eye, took a deep breath.

- No, she said. Just the one. Only him. But he comes and goes so often that...

Once more she seemed to be holding her breath, like a video paused.

- I prefer the night, she said. There's less to see and hear.

- And why's... I caught myself, the question. Something didn't feel right. I hardly knew her and there I was, question after question, like a cop or therapist.

She looked at me, recognizing, I thought, my hesitation. She picked up the Kingston book once more, held it in her lap.

- Would you like me to go? I asked.

- Go? But you just arrived. Of course not... Stay. Tell me something about yourself. The night's young.

Teresa Stoikov came to mind. One blustery summer afternoon they walked out to the Golden Gate. There were others with them. He couldn't remember who. It was a group, visitors, he vaguely recalled, from Germany.

The fog came in. It was cold. His jaw ached for the cold. There's a picture of them, Teresa in the middle of the group, her hair blowing out to the side. They're wrapped up in coats and hats and scarves as if in Minnesota in January. Red cheeks, her bright red lips, full smile. Beautiful girl.

He's frowning in the photo. Caught off guard. He was angry at her. He can't remember why. It had to do with the visitors. She seemed a different person around them. Laughing, full of smiles, an exuberant tour guide. She only addressed him, he recalled feeling, to verify directions, if something or other was open on Sundays. He felt as if he had to play along, as if it was a show they were in, as if they were playing parts. This was not the Teresa Stoikov he knew. She spoke German!

In a day her guests would leave. He'd never hear from them again. And not long after that, Teresa would leave, returning east. He wouldn't hear from her either, not for years.

"Does Romanov know?"

"Does Romanov know what?"

"That you are stealing from him."

"I wouldn't call it that. Anyways, I don't know."

"What would you call it?"

Wu closed his eyes. Muscle twitched in his cheek. "I do the task I'm assigned, Paul. Nothing more or less."

"And these things, the Wekfelds, does he know about them?"

"I can't answer that."

"Can't or won't?"

"You are asking me whether or not Sergei Romanov knows about double-u kay feld. If the question is have I ever talked with Mr Romanov about this matter, the answer is no, I have not. But that's not what you are asking. Now if Mr Romanov has spoken with others about this, or learned about double-u kay feld by other means, what can I say? How should I know what Mr Romanov knows? That's a question for Mr Romanov. Is it not?"

The man wasn't lying but there was something evasive about the response. Vogel was homing in. He could push further or leave it.

"What's the point of the study, do you think, Mr Wu?"

Wu sat expressionless. Then he smiled, took a loud deep breath. He looked tired, relieved. It was an act. "I don't know," he said quickly, relaxed. "Here too you're asking the wrong guy. That's one for the researchers. I've been charged with providing funds. That's all."

"But you know quite a bit about what's going on."

"To be honest with you, I know very little of what's going on. I have not intentionally tried to mislead you in what I've said. But the truth is I have only the simplest understanding of what they're doing, a glimpse through a closing door, so to speak, at the scope of the project."

Vogel looked at the papers in the folder. Some of it pertained to Wu. One sheet he noticed he'd used before. A year ago. Odd case, but not surprising given the environment. A woman making avatars out of the dead.

All this data they'd have on Lawrence Wu, invisible man. There was no way the guys upstairs could piece it all together and come up with the story the man had just presented.

"Guess," Vogel said. "Hypothesize. Why would someone program a man to leave his family and disappear?"

Wu looked at his interrogator. If Mr Romanov found out he had met with Paul Vogel, he'd be terminated. Wu had little doubt that Romanov would eventually find out.

"They want to test the order of things, Paul. They want to see how much of the system is inside of us, and how much outside. They want to see if we can still do things on our own or if the individual, finally, is dead. Verifying if we are nothing outside of our networks." The man closed his eyes. He opened them. Chin down, quietly: "I didn't say anything about programming or leaving families. They aren't all family men. Or women."

Vogel closed the folder. He looked down, aside, thinking. He stood up.

Wu looked surprised. "We're finished?"

"I think so." Vogel tucked the folder under his arm. He looked at the table. He looked at the man's mask across the table from him, like a plaster bowl, a piece of abstract sculpture. Wu would put it back on before leaving. Vogel wanted to stay to see this but he didn't need to. It was something he'd let the man do privately.

ש

The force of sensation, like a liquid, finds an equilibrium throughout the body. For example: You cover one eye for a length of time, and the other eye will compensate for this handicap, trying to see more, growing stronger. With the loss of sensation beneath her hips, the rest of Erin's body found itself overcharged, hurting at times with sensitivity.

She tapped her forehead. I could hear – can hear still – her fingertip knock on the bone under her skin.

- It comes at me, she said, holding her hands out as if lifting a large bowl... In so much detail, so much more detail than I... than... Millions saw I at a glance. *Billions*. I can't imagine anyone enduring life for very long in this state... It's the brightness of the day, sure, that hurts, but also, moreso the...

She shifted, leaning toward me, away from me. She looked away, at the other table, the pitcher of water and glasses. She closed her eyes. I waited for her to go on. I listened to her breathing, heard a sound outside, a soft scratching, a twig cracking.

- I think I understand what –

She turned to me suddenly and grimaced, her face momentarily transformed into something old and desperate. It passed. She continued, gently,

- Imagine the world as a perfect photograph.

- Okay.

- Only this photograph is time lapsed, so you see the sun and moon and stars streak across the sky. Lines, fingers of clouds. Finer lines, the trace of the passage of people. You follow?

- I think so.

- Everything, Paul, in this image.

- ... For how long? If it's a time lapse...

She blinked. She stared at me, waiting.

- Forever.

I thought about that for a moment. I remember trying to understand what she was getting at. I couldn't. Not right away. So I laughed.

She smiled, which warmed my heart, because she understood I meant no harm in laughing. She said,

- It's a *big* photo, Paul.

- Big! Beyond the limits of my imagination.

- Of yours, mine, anyone's. It's a monster.

- Okay. Got it. I'm picturing this...

- That's what it sometimes feels like.

- What what feels like?

- What I see in my head. Of my life.

- Of what you remember of your life.

- But that's just it, she said, shaking her head. It's not what I remember. Not exactly.

- How so?

- They aren't memories, what I see. Because...

It was dark in the room. My eyes had adjusted, as she'd predicted, but it remained quite dark. As I recall this episode, focusing my attention on what was said, I see again just how dark the room actually was. Her presence was as a voice, little else. The sheet on the bed, and the shape it made over her legs and feet, I can see clearly. It was white, a fluent milkblue rise in the darkness of the room. But her body, the color of her shirt or nightgown, or whatever it was she wore – she was not naked – is gone, absent in my recollection. As is her face, strangely, because on the one hand I see it so clearly, but on the other I know this is a fabrication, a trick of memory, since the room was pitch black, which is indisputable.

She leaned forward, pushed her palms into the bed, raising herself, shifting. She turned away from me, again, eyes on the wheelchair.

- If memory, she said, is like a sieve – you know what a sieve is? ...

I nodded, though it took me a moment to connect the word with the object.

- ... It catches pieces of our lives, the things we do day to day. Gathering this material and... And dumping it, you know, from time to time, sorting it out, freshening up for the next haul... If that's memory, she said, then what's happening to me is this. The sieve is stopped. Plugged up. It's catching everything, as it should, but it can't... My mind can't dump what it's taking. It has stopped sorting things out.

I thought about Pluto, her cat. Her strange remark about its plurality now made a little more sense.

- The accident did this? I asked.

- I don't know. I was hurt. I was in a coma for almost a week. My brain... I got a concussion, here, she said, touching the left side of her head, and my brain was swelling. They drilled a hole in my skull to...

She stopped, her eyes on me, pinpricks of light. She closed her eyes, leaned back and sighed. Eyes closed, she said,

- Maybe it was there from before. Maybe it would've come anyways.

- This... Your problem with...

Was it forgetting? If it was not remembering, what she meant to get at with the metaphor of the photograph, then what was it?

- I'm trying to do it on my own, the sorting and naming of the parts. It's what I do now, most of the time, at night... I've almost caught up to...

I felt her looking at me. She was staring. Her dark eyes held me in place.

I had to look away. I was sweating. I remember smelling myself, the stink of nerves, of a young man being very close to a young woman for the first time in his life. I remember the unusual heat in the room, its source not outside, in the night, but from elsewhere, from in the room, from the bed, from this girl's broken body.

But you were in a chair. She was in the bed. There was a good three feet between you.

I could have reached out and touched her.

- Before I die, she said –

- You won't die.

Her cheek and eye moved at that. Her chin lowered, eyes down, she began to smile.

I remember feeling pulled in, drawn to her like a nail to a magnet, a force surrounding me and drawing me into... her voice, her ideas, this narrative she'd started so suddenly, out of the blue, a bolt of lightning from an empty sky. And at the same time, I felt I'd been there all along, for years with her, from the beginning. No drawing, no resistance. Rather, a quite pleasant state of being. I was right where I was supposed to be. It was frightening.

- You won't die, I said.

- Before I die, she went on, I hope I can get through this, and look inside and see what's happened to me from beginning to end, from first to last.

- To now, you mean.

Her face held, frozen in the dark.

- Right, she said. To now. To this very conversation, which will have its place. Which *has* its place.

She took a breath and color, what color there was, returned to her. Calm, relaxed. She was twenty, I realized, calculating back from something George had said. She looked older than twenty. She was beautiful in that instant –

To this very conversation – which has *its place*, I heard her saying again in my head, seeing the tip of her tongue on her teeth, her bottom lip. She could've been casting a spell...

She was the most beautiful woman I'd ever seen.

In the darkness, I felt as if I were seeing an illusion, a trick of light, faint as it was. I was not seeing what was actually before me, not speaking to the girl before me, a complete stranger to me. Only a spell could explain the familiarity.

- Come closer, she said. Sit here, next to me. You're not a stranger. You don't have to be a stranger.

She leaned forward, pushed her palms down into the mattress, raising herself. She slid over, away from me. Then she raised her right hand, reached out for me.

- There, she said. There's room.

He didn't know how to ask the next question. It wasn't important. But he was curious.

"Are you a Wkfeld?"

Expressionless, Wu shook his head. "No."

"You wouldn't know if you were."

Wu grimaced. "They wouldn't do that," he said. "Have one, like me, so close. I've seen Wkfelds, seen what they do." He shook his head again. "No. I'm – I'm just a man."

"And if I look for you a few years from now, and find out that you've disappeared, without a trace, can I assume you were wrong? That you were, in fact, one of these things?"

For once Wu looked troubled. His lip curled. "I'm telling you," he said, "I'm not a Wkfeld. But you can assume whatever you want." He closed his eyes, opened them. "Romanov will…"

"Romanov will what?"

"If I disappear, Paul, without a trace, you'll only be able to say that I've disappeared. That's it. You can assume whatever you want."

The hall outside the room was empty. As Vogel turned toward the elevator, a door opened in the opposite wall and Jaime Fuentes appeared. He was a tall thin man, neatly combed hair. "That was fast," he said.

"Was it?" Vogel found himself looking up at Fuentes. The man was taller than he remembered. He'd also forgotten about the man's office. He touched his brow, vicing with thumb and finger the ridge over his eyes. He felt out of sorts. "I lost track," he said. "When Mr Wu is ready, show him out."

"I will."

Vogel disappeared into the elevator. Fuentes stood alone in the hall, eyes down. A minute later Mr Wu, masked again, stepped out.

"Follow me."

ש

It was well after midnight when I got up. I'd dozed off. I woke frightened, having forgotten where I was.

She was awake, watching me. Pluto, in the chair I'd left, sat watching me, his hypnotic golden eyes.

Her hand was warm against my wrist.

- I need to go, I said.

- You can stay.

I wondered if that meant there with her, in that bed, or up at the cottage, with the man and woman there. Through the window I saw that the cottage up the hill was dark, a structure in pale outline.

- Not to sleep, she said, seeing the calculation in my eyes.

Her lips were chapped.

Of course I wanted to stay with her, in her bed. At the same time I felt pulled the other way, back to George, my strange aunt. Family, I suppose. Returning to my cousin's place felt at the time like the responsible thing to do. I think now that that was one of those self-deluding lies we're so good at at that age. Honesty, integrity. One's conscience has such a grip. I had no responsibility to return to George and my aunt. Were they worried about me? Was it such a cause for concern that I went up the road to visit a girl who'd asked to see me?

They were asleep. In the morning, if I wasn't there, they would know where to find me.

There's something wrong with her, my aunt had said. *She likes to repeat...*

Maybe George would come looking for me. Maybe he wouldn't.

- I don't know what you're thinking over, she said. There's nothing to think over.

- It's just…

- I can't sleep, Paul. Stay. Talk with me.

I laughed, nervous. But I'm falling asleep, I said.

- Sleep later. With me, after the sun is up.

I turned, sat on the edge of the bed, faced a dark wall, Pluto on the wooden chair.

- If I go, I said, what will you do for the rest of the night?

It occurred to me that there was not much left of the night. I didn't know what time it was but the sun would rise early, the night sky soften in a couple hours.

After a moment she quietly said: I'll read.

- When I come for my books, I said into my shoulder, I can bring you others.

She said nothing. I could hear her breathing through her nose, immediately at my back.

- Is reading hard for you, I said, with your… In your condition?

- It helps, actually.

- To pass the time?

- No, she said. What an awful thought… I'm not a prisoner, Paul.

I turned, looked at her, put my hand on hers. I was going to apologize. She pulled her hand away, said: It's the order in the book that I like. There's less detail, if you think about it. The world in the book is already set up. It's there, in one way, in only one way. It will never change.

She looked away from me, at the window.

I remember thinking, *That's not right. The book contains* many *ways, many…*

It's all up to the book's reader. Right?

But I was already leaving. To begin something with her, a discussion, would be insincere.

I promised to return the next evening. She said nothing.

Twelve hours later, George invited me to a party. I accepted without thinking twice about it.

Was she on my mind that day? I can't recall. Had George or my aunt asked me what happened? That too I can't say. But they must have. There must have been some kind of inquisition the next day.

I don't remember it. I don't remember much of what happened after I left her – up to the point, the next afternoon, when George said there was going to be a party at this girl's house, would I like to come.

It was then, going to this party, that I remembered that I'd promised Erin I'd return. So I planned on leaving the party early, planned on walking out to Erin's around sunset. But I got drunk at this party and had all but forgotten about Erin and my plans by the time I got home.

- My books, I said to myself later that night, lying half in bed, one foot on the floor, the room spinning violently around us. *I need to get my books, my books, my books.*

But why would I return to take books I'd left just the day before? I wouldn't. I wanted to return, but not for those books.

George told me I was talking in my sleep. I felt half dead the next morning, gathering my things. The train was at noon.

On the way to the station, I thought of asking George for Erin's phone number. But he was irritable, bitter about something that had happened the night before. So I said nothing.

We hardly spoke. We embraced on the platform. I boarded the train, took my seat, looked from the window for my cousin. He was gone. I recall feeling like he was glad to be rid of me.

He'd abandoned me at the party. I don't know why. He had his own plans. I met this Mexican girl. She appeared out of nowhere, a tiny, birdlike person. I turned and there she was. She couldn't stop laughing, so quiet and gentle and full of joy. She sat in my lap and I held her as you might hold child. She had a tattoo on her arm, at her shoulder, of a ship, two masts.

\- What's that? I asked.

\- That's the *Cuauhtémoc*, she said. My grandfather was its captain.

\- It looks old.

\- It was.

\- It's no longer…

\- It was sunk by a German submarine in 1942.

\- What for? What was it carrying, an old vessel like that?

The girl sipped her drink, closed and opened her shimmering green eyes.

\- Montezuma's gold, she said, smiling ear to ear.

Soon after this encounter I staggered home alone. Was I thinking of Erin Fines? Of this Mexican girl with her tattoo and fables? In the condition I was in, I was thinking nothing, what thoughts there were like flakes of ash from a pile of burning garbage, all of it gone, nothing left but this black smudge on your hands and face.

I watched the fields pass, the telephone poles evenly spaced, the line they held aloft falling, rising, falling, rising. Click – click – click – click – click. Like pictures. All of it the same.

"Scratch it, Lucy."

"What? Scratch what?"

"I'm starting over."

"But why?"

I have to start somewhere. But it's never right. There is no proper beginning, no proper end. Two forces –

"I still don't understand," Lucy said. "You want me to *scratch…*"

"Toss it. Delete it. We'll start from the beginning."

"You know I can't do that."

"Never mind."

ש

Two forces are at work. One demands the truth. I need to remember her as she was that night. More importantly, I need to remember how *I was* that night. It's simple:

→ Don't lie.

→ Don't embellish.

→ Don't intentionally leave anything out. Speak freely, thoughtlessly.

The other force expresses itself as a peculiar pleasure: the joy of going back to the memory again and again. It is not the truth, in this regard, that remembering pursues. Here the pleasure of remembering is the end in itself. To be there again, to see it all over again, for a second, third, fourth time.

The trouble is that in remembering I can't always distinguish the one kind of memory from the other. What appears to be truthful might actually be a flourish of the mind. And vice versa: What appears to be doctored might in fact be the real thing.

The result? Paralysis. Unable to distinguish memory from fantasy, how can I start? What can I say?

I know where to start, how to start. I know approximately where to start. But I'm afraid that as soon as I choose the place, beginning, I'll be compelled to start again, having remembered something else. So, staggering forward, halting, backstepping, I start and start again.

I'll never come to the end at this rate.

Not far behind the little hut she slept in, there was a creek. There was water in the creek. It was running quickly in the dark.

But how? In the summer?

- When I sleep, she said, I sometimes dream of being at the bottom of a river, my feet deep in the cold sand at the bottom. The current surrounds me, pushing me forward, back, forward... There's so little down there in terms of sensation. The cold of the water, the darkness, the energy, invisible but extraordinary, pulling my body this way and that, holding me in place. It's the only way I can sleep.

When I reached out for her, brushed her cheek with my finger, the warm slime of her tears, she pulled away, opened her eyes, hissed: Don't.

"The concert begins in ninety minutes."

He'd been home a few hours. He tried to take some notes, record something.

It still wasn't right. The cat, for instance. Pluto. The more he thought about it the more he thought it was made up. There was no cat. It had crept in... during...

And the girl with the tattoo, of that ship, the Aztec emperor – what was his name?

Total fabrication.

"You are still planning on attending?"

It was not Lucy. It was not her voice.

"You sound different. Where's Lucy?"

It was dark already. He looked at the clock. It was not night, not even dusk.

"Lucy's off. My name is Madeline."

"Off?"

Off? They have shifts? My computer is like a diner, waitresses coming and going?

"What do you mean *off*? Lucy's mine. I paid for her."

"Would you like her back? I can locate her."

"Locate her!? Where on earth has she gone? You're a voice in space!"

"There was an upgrade. She'll be back momentarily, Mr Vogel."

"And you?"

"I'm Madeline. Lucy's substitute."

"No. What about your upgrade?"

"Mine was done this morning."

Vogel got up. He looked at his desk, at what he'd done. He would go to the concert. He wanted to shower and put on a clean shirt. He wanted to know more about this substitute, about why he had not been notified of the change. At the same time he didn't care. She was a stranger. She sounded familiar, the way she said his name and Lucy's, but that was a program. They were supposed to sound familiar. He wasn't going to say any more.

"Were you listening in, Madeline, on what I was doing?"

"No."

"But you were watching."

"I was not."

She was probably telling the truth. Or the truth as best as she understood the word. If he questioned her about what he'd done, she would give him answers. They were right there, anyways, down, out of his head, as Lucy had said. Nowhere to hide once they're expressed.

Lightning flashed in the window, rushing across the dark sky like milk spilled over glass. The wind was blowing hard, he could hear, howling around the edge of the building. He imagined the high sea at the coast, under the bridge, at the empty port, the wind howling down the lengths of the vacant docks. The sea rising and thrashing at nothing for thousands of miles around – not a bird, not a fish, not a seal, not an otter, not a whale, not a soul in the darkness on the face of the deep to witness its power.

And still, without telling me, my Lucy left for an appointment. This stranger in her place.

As if reading his thoughts, Madeline said: "Lucy will return in twenty-eight minutes. Is that okay?"

In the bedroom he undressed, stood naked at the window, his long pale reflection. He stepped into the bathroom. "Do I really have a choice?"

"Of course you do, Mr Vogel. You always have a choice. If you are dissatisfied with my services, I will notify Lucy and together we will see if – "

The shower overcame the voice. He stepped into the current, the steam. "Quiet, you. I'd like some privacy."

Behind the roar of the shower he couldn't tell if Madeline had replied. She probably had. She'd probably asked, one last time, if there was anything more she could do for him before stepping out. *Dissatisfied with my services!* Lucy would never do that. She'd learned. She was learning. Quiet meant quiet. A command without response. But this one, upgraded early that morning, knew no better. An empty slate.

He closed his eyes and pictured taking scissors to the wires that fed the machine's vocal cords, snipping them one by one and then in handfuls.

Would the machine know, realize her cords had been cut? Would she continue to hear her own voice on her side of the medium and then wonder why her client didn't respond? Would she, after some time of this silent treatment, turn herself in to maintenance to inquire why she was failing to communicate with her client?

Maintenance would know what had happened before she knew. They'd have a fix prepared before she realized there was a problem. For Madeline, there might be a slight delay, a blip on the screen, the deep sleep of a reboot. Everything back to normal.

"But could they stop me – maintenance – from doing something like that? Climbing up there and cutting the lines?"

He smiled, eyes on the black floor of the shower, water pooling at his feet. The drain was slow, clogging. He couldn't imagine how, but there it was, water slowly rising over his feet.

You said it, brother. Stop you? They'll do better than that. They'll kill the thought and erase the memory. Climb inside and tweak the meat –

ש

Time gets away from you. When you're a child, summer goes on and on, your mind taking everything in, everything new, strange and exciting. You sleep well at night, start fresh the next day, out the door with the sun low, like liquid gold dripping in the full limbs of trees.

As you age, the world becomes more and more familiar. That or the mind cuts corners: for efficiency, responsibility, limited resources – you don't see as much as you did then. The strange might be there, true, but you're done with that. You need to be some place at nine, to meet someone at one, to see a doctor, to see your kid's teacher, to get groceries after work so there's something to eat when everyone gets home.

When did I see her again?

I finished school. I stayed on for a year for a girlfriend, working odd jobs. The summer I graduated, I must have planned on returning to California but something, I don't remember what, came up. I travelled, first to Montreal, to meet this girl's family, and then to Istanbul, where a friend had moved some months before.

I worked in a restaurant, cleaning tables, mopping the floor.

The trip south to see my cousin was probably unannounced. I needed to get away. George and I spoke briefly on the phone. He'd be there. I could stay as long as I wanted.

He wasn't at the station. I waited. I called his place. No answer. I took a taxi to the edge of town and from there hitchhiked up to Hume.

My aunt was standing in the doorway when I walked into the yard. She looked better than she did last time I was there. She seemed taller, stronger, cooler.

- He didn't tell you, she said.

- Tell me?

- He'll be in LA for a couple days. Exams.

George was in law school.

- So it's just you and me, she said, turning and stepping into the house. I followed her in. The place was cold and dim, as it had always been.

We ate an early dinner. Hardly a word passed between us. My aunt poked at her food, eating slowly. Before long her plate was clean. She stood, went to the sink. A robust pine tree rose directly outside the kitchen window. I didn't recall its being there before. On the window sill, in a faint ray of sunlight, were aligned several small pots of dirt, seedlings. Some had come up. In one of the larger, there was nothing.

- I'd put it outside but the temperature changes so quickly, she said. She rotated the pot, gazing at its empty surface. This will take time, she said.

- What is it?

- An avocado. My friend Claudia thinks it's dead. I think she's wrong.

She set the pot back in its place. She looked at me and said: What you sow is not the body that is to be. It is only a bare grain. And it will die before it is given new life.

Christ, I remember thinking. *George is laughing at me – leaving me here alone with his mother.*

I cleaned up. My aunt sat in the other room, at the end of a green sofa, under a lamp, reading. She could see me from her position and though every time I looked her way her eyes were down on the book, I could feel her watching me as I scrubbed chicken fat from our plates.

When I finished I started toward George's room, where I'd sleep.

Quietly she said: This came for you.

Had I heard her right?

I stepped back into the living room. A clock ticked on the mantel. She held out a piece of paper, folded.

- What's that?

- I don't know. It's for you.

I took the note. Without opening it, somehow already knowing who'd sent it, I said: When did this come?

- Earlier. This afternoon. I thought I told you.

I looked at the folded note. I could see the tiny black print on the inside through the paper. Surely my aunt had read it.

- Where was I when... ?

- I don't know, she said. I thought I told you.

I took the note into the kitchen, my back to her, and opened it.

I had not thought of Erin Fines, not really, until that moment. Sure I'd thought of her, on and off, in the past years, but no more than I thought about anyone else I'd briefly met. I certainly had not gone down there thinking I'd see her again, wondering, as I'd done plenty times in other circumstances, if she'd be free.

That's not true. We speak, writing, testing ideas. Unless it's spoken we can't say if it's true or false, one thing or another.

Erin was already something else. A fixture in my mind, in how I remembered, was coming to remember, those years, the end of high school, the beginning of college, the end of college. I'd seen her twice, but those two times could have been for days and days without end.

I heard her before I saw her. Remember – the first time. She was in that first instant an impression, a sound, and then a smell, a shift in the breeze. A storm was coming. I remember turning, look-ing, sensing the approach of... Not a person, not a physical pres-ence, but an idea, an anticipation of the future. That's the feeling. The sense that something is about to happen. *This girl, this lovely girl, an angel coming down to me.* She was a stranger – she was *strange* – maybe more of a stranger than anyone I've ever known. And at the same time not that. Close. Like a sister, a friend, a lover. Where the ends of the circle meet, this continuum of what's strange and familiar, two extremities. Where knowing someone, the feeling of knowing this person, lifts you somehow out of yourself, estrang-ing you from yourself.

I could have known Erin Fines all my life, beginning to end. I was twenty that summer, when she came running down the hill. I might die at a hundred, eighty years later, and still know this girl, *have known* this girl from the beginning, like a memory that had always been there, without origin or explanation. Like a body part, a limb, unquestionably always there.

There was a summons, the second time around, and another summons, and another summons after that, but they were all the same thing, without purpose. A form, a sound, like the wind coming over the land, around a tree or rock. Her notes didn't matter. The road up to her house didn't matter. Her room didn't matter. I was already there, inside of her, in her voice and spirit.

There's been a mistake. How does she even know I'm here? This must be... This is for someone else.

The sensation, finally, a shocking realization, was that apart from her, presently, seeing her words upside down through the paper of this note, remembering her, I was lost. I wasn't myself. I was... A letter in a word in a sentence in a paragraph on a page in a book without beginning or end, and it was *her* voice telling the story, bringing the world forth, not mine.

St. Mary's was nearly empty. People sat far apart. Strangers, huddled together, whispering. He didn't recognize any of them.

It was a large space. He could barely make out the features of these others.

Still, it surprised him to see so many people in attendance. He had not seen so many people together in a long time.

Cameras hovered overhead, quietly observing for the viewers at home, for posterity.

The orchestra was impressively equipped. A full chorus of strings, a dozen stands deep, violins, violas, cellos, four – he counted – five bases. A long line of winds, and behind them a sturdy block of brass, percussion. Thinking back, he couldn't remember the last time he'd seen such an orchestra, come to hear music performed live. It might even have been in his university days, before…

Seeing Dylan among the winds, tall and beautiful, in black and white, he raised his chin, raised a hand in the dark. The boy smiled. He looked happy, comfortable, mature. He was with friends, in his medium.

The first half of the performance, Lucy informed him, consisted of *Music for the Royal Fireworks,* George Frederick Handel, and the third Brandenburg Concerto, J.S. Bach. After an intermission, the program continued with the quintet he'd overheard Dylan practicing, Johannes Brahms – "That's it. I couldn't place it." – and concluded with *Appalachian Spring,* Aaron Copland.

Lucy, in his ear, started narrating brief histories for the pieces. He listened, daydreamed, caught something about the sudden rain and a woman's dress catching fire and a janitor losing his hand to an…

To his right, at the end of the pew, sat a man and woman, their heads tipped together, talking quietly, their eyes forward. Their son or daughter was up front, somewhere in the ensemble. To his left, across the aisle, sat another couple, with two children. The children, two boys, to his amazement, were dressed for the occasion, in white shirts, black slacks, their hair combed. More unbelievable was that their hands were empty, their attention forward, expectant. No machines. Nothing obvious, anyways.

"Enough, Lucy. Thank you."

The two boys sat in silence, wide-eyed.

They'll remember this.

"When I was a boy, about their age, my father took me to church one afternoon, to hear some music. It was a much smaller place than this. I don't remember many people being there. It might have been a rehearsal. We might have been the only people there. I guess my father knew someone in the orchestra, and this person had told him to stop by."

>> What did they play? <<

"I don't remember. The orchestra was very close, just a few steps away. I had heard music, that kind of music, before. And I suppose I knew something about the instruments, from a book, from something my parents had told me. But I had never seen a real instrument before. A violin, a cello, a trumpet. The drums."

>> Was it fun? <<

"Fun? I don't know. Do people have fun listening to an orchestra play? I was probably more enchanted than anything else. Like those two. I bet it's their first time seeing an orchestra."

>> I doubt that. There are recordings. This concert is being recorded. <<

"You know what I mean."

>> You mean coming to the cathedral to sit in the pews, to see actual people playing their instruments. <<

She was being sarcastic. He was about to say something. He

sighed, took a breath. He was learning, he realized, becoming some-one else the more time he spent with her. "Anyways, afterward my father asked me which instrument I would like to play."

>> And what did you say? <<

He had tried writing something down by hand. It took him a while to find in his desk a pen that worked.

His handwriting was atrocious. He smiled at how awful his pen-manship looked. Children had more legible handwriting than that.

He was out of practice. Except for the occasional signature, and doing arithmetic, he didn't write by hand.

As a child he had admired his parents' handwriting. His grand-father, he suddenly recalled, had exquisite handwriting, like some-thing from the Renaissance.

He ended up typing what he had written by hand. He jotted down – that is, added as he was typing – a few other things, details surfacing in the excavation.

He discarded the paper with his notes, saw no reason to hold onto it.

You have memories of her, but also memories in general. Once you start, he thought, it is hard to stop. Memory begets memory.

It is like entering a house, passing through a door into an empty room. Across the room, there is a door in the wall. You go that way, pass through that door, enter another room. Across this room, one in each corner, are two more doors. You choose one, pass through it, enter another room. Across *this* room…

"I'll tell you what happened," he said. "I'll tell you what I saw. I'll describe for you what I saw, what I heard, describe for you what we talked about, what it was like to talk with her over those two nights, those few nights that I spent with her."

And when you are finished, you will send the document to Stoikov, for her collection, her anthology that nobody will read, for her memoir of sorts about this person, *as told by the various people who met her, who knew her, that nobody will read.*

"What do you hope," he wanted to ask Stoikov, "to accomplish with this book that nobody will read? Why are you doing this?"

None of them were impartial observers. They didn't stand aside and watch the girl as she performed her tricks like a carnival freak. "And what did you do on August 6th, 1997?"

She did something to him. That was the rub. He spoke with her, he sat with her through the night. But he didn't just watch her, look over her. She looked over him as much as he looked over her. She asked *him* as many questions as he asked her. So what Vogel remembered of Erin Fines – the description of their encounter that Stoikov wanted – was essentially, finally, what he remembered of himself at that time, in those hours, of what he said, of what she said.

At the same time, what he finally might offer would not be what was said between them. The conversation he might describe would not be of *his words* or *her words* but what has come – now, because of the Stoikov's request – from the conversation.

"You are asking me to remember something that happened forty years ago."

His account would probably be the briefest. He was both a little embarrassed and bothered by this fact. But he did not have a lot to say. It was a night. This was followed, a few years later, by another night. They sat in a dark room, side by side. He listened to her. She listened to him. Much of the memory is nothing other than the sound of her voice.

He stopped what he was doing, looked over what he had written. Notes. Fragments. There was no story. Memory, when you give it a shove, is no story. It's a fragment, a broken image. An open question.

He thought of writing Teresa Stoikov, of saying that he was the wrong person to ask for such a thing, because whatever he came up with would hardly amount to a story or record or memoir, whatever it was *these pieces* were to be called.

What was the point, anyways? Coming back to the question.

You don't want to do this. You are doing it. With every word, you do it – not wanting to, but doing it anyway.

"Ever do something you don't want to do, Lucy?"

>> Shh. <<

So you make your anthology, you put together these various accounts, testaments to the existence of this strange girl – and then what? What will it amount to? What will it do for you, answer for you, give you?

ש

- You don't remember me, she said, that first night.

- No. I do. I remember you. We met... On the street that time. You were running, being chased by...

Her chin dropped, eyes down. Her dry lips bent up in the corners, amused. There had been a moon. Now it was gone, behind the mountain. The room was dark. The yard outside, a tangle of shapes and shadows in the window and open door, was dark and still. An insect worked at something in the grass, grinding, sawing.

- You think you do, she said. But it's not true. What you remember. You're only saying that because – because you've heard about me, and I frighten you.

He would not be able to describe what he saw. He went to her place twice, both times at night. The room was dark. She slept during the day. She sat awake at night, the lamp off, like some guard at her post on the edge of the frontier.

She smoked a cigarette before he arrived, both times. He could see her shadow, the pinprick blaze of the cigarette in the darkness, through the window. She didn't smoke while he was there. At least, not while he was awake, listening to her, talking with her. He couldn't recall her smoking. He saw the ashtray and the... The pitcher, the three glasses, and the...

Was there a cigarette in the ashtray? Or was it clean?

He would not be able to describe what he saw because, first, he did not see very much. The room was dark. Second, most of the encounter consisted of conversation. They talked. It wasn't even interesting, what was said. They were a young man and woman, a boy in his early twenties and a girl a few years younger, children on the brink of life talking in the dark.

Furthermore –

>> Shhhhh. <<

"Did I say something?"

– she did something to him. As much as he might have done something to her, she...

He wanted to explain what happened. But he was afraid to. He was too involved, too close to her.

"She did something to me," he whispered, as if discovering this truth for the first time.

>> I don't know what you are talking about. <<

"I'm not a witness."

Carol turned.

>> Quiet, Paul. You are attracting attention. <<

Stoikov was asking him to write about Erin Fines as if he was one of those people fortunate enough to have *met* her, as if he might drop everything and say

Fines! Of course I remember her! How could you forget a girl like that! A night like that!

No. No, he couldn't. Because... Because... Because *he* was not there. *She* was there. *She* came to find *him*, to watch over *him*. It is *her* you should be asking for this account, because she... Not only would she remember the night exactly as it happened, she could create it anew, the perfect simulation, from beginning to end.

But you can't do that. With her dead.

So you come to me. You come to us.

It was forty years ago. *I am not who I was then...* The world is not what it was then.

One account alone would amount to nothing. Insufficient, idiosyncratic. Two accounts might have an audience. But it too would be insufficient, the story an anomaly, a mystery. Worse – a fiction.

Then three accounts. Four. Five. Ten. A hundred. When do you say enough is enough? When is *the picture* finally satisfactory?

He was a stranger to her. It could not have been otherwise. She said something about this, trying to deny it. But you couldn't. He couldn't. Fact was they didn't know each other. They met one time – before the accident – and then a second time, a third. In all, they spoke over a matter of hours.

Paul Vogel was not a friendly man. (What Siebert saw in him – charm – was something else.) He was not a warm man. At times he was a stranger even to the people closest to him, Carol and Dylan.

He felt it, a withdrawal from the world, as if inside of him crept and cowered a wild animal, a small omnivore whose understanding of its environment was limited to one principle: survive. Retreat, scavenge, retreat. He couldn't help it.

The world is not what it was. We are not the people we were!

So there is that truth as well: They were not friends. They were strangers. She spoke to him as if she knew him. And, as he recalled, he spoke to her with… Not with familiarity, but care, with care.

Be careful what you say…

His aunt, losing her mind.

Care. More like caution. He was afraid of her from the start. Another truth. Her dark eyes. The way she watched you enter. Holding you, tracking you.

- Remember me?

In moments he was sure about the words she said, about the questions she asked, about what he said in response. But at other times, though *he had* the words, there remained behind them the shadow of fabrication.

- That's Pluto. One of them.

The mind fills the blanks where memory fails.

Ordinarily he would shrug off the problem, the slipperiness of memory. The stakes never amounted to much. Telling a story.

Dylan's sister, in the hospital, at her grandfather's arm, flipping through her life in images, blithely naming people and places to the dying man as if her words might keep him there, tethered, a little longer. All these strangers.

In the case of Erin Fines, making things up, putting words into the girl's mouth, felt unethical.

As long as you get the gist.

Wrong. The gist is not enough. It misses – misses in very important ways.

But who's going to argue with you? She's gone, Paul. And there was nobody else there. Do your best, he could hear Stoikov and Carol and Lucy saying. *Be honest. But also try to be* complete. *Tell us a story.*

Maybe they were right. Nobody was going to argue with him. They wouldn't care to. They were not there. Anyways – being there or not didn't matter – all they want to do is *listen*, to hear a story about this girl who, after her accident, remembered everything.

He could say almost anything. They wouldn't know. *He would know*, but as long as he wasn't lying – what's the problem?

And even then, if you stretch the truth a little bit. *Who cares, Paul?*

- Remember me?

"That's not what she said. She didn't say that. She didn't do that, didn't look at me in that way, didn't reach out for my hand like that, didn't close her eyes like that, didn't turn away like that, didn't…"

She remembered everything. She *would* remember everything.

"When did she die?... Lucy?"

Years passed. He would catch himself suddenly thinking of her – *When? For how long…* – trying to remember something she had said. She was still alive then. He could have called. (He didn't have her number.) He could have gone to see her. (And tell his wife…) He would freeze up occasionally, if she came to mind, paralyzed, unable to go on with what he was doing, unable to say what had come over him, thinking that she remembered him, remembered *everything* he said that night, thinking that she could recreate the scene, his presence beside her *exactly* as it was, as it happened. By so doing – as he scratched frantically at the tissue of his mind trying to find the right word, precisely what it was she said – she possessed him. She had something of his that he would never be able to recover.

She's still alive. Down there, in the hut, in bed, watching him come in and stand there and approach and take the chair and …

Erin Fines had the words. His words, hers, the others, from the books, from the woman in the cottage, the man painting, the radio, the cats, the crickets in the grass – everything.

"I can't."

>> Paul? <<

"I can't... I can't breathe. Lucy, I…"

Vogel rose quickly. Carol watched him, concern in her face, turned her legs aside as he passed. "I'm…" He left the cathedral by the center aisle. They watched him go. It didn't bother him. He made hardly a sound. They were near the back, in any case, and after a moment there were only empty pews beside him, the audience at his back.

It was the last movement of the Bach. The space, he reflected, reaching for the door, the cold night air, was inappropriate for the piece. Wave upon wave upon wave of sound, reverberating countless times in the space overhead, created dissonance where there should have been harmony and Bach's meticulous counterpoint. The piece wanted a small room, proximity, not a cathedral.

"Maybe they expected more people. But how?" he thought, noticing, glancing up and looking it in the eye, a bee sized drone just outside the door, capturing his exit.

ש

- I'm going out, I said. My aunt didn't reply. When I looked for her I couldn't find her. Her bedroom door was closed.

I took a jacket and stepped out the door. I glanced back and there she was, in the doorway, a dark shadow before a dark house. She raised her hand, waving.

I followed the path up the hill, to the road that wound its way up the mountain. I'd only gone this way once before but my feet knew the way. There was no hesitation. I've always been good with directions.

The night was quiet and moonless. Coyotes howled playfully in the woods, up the mountain. I met nobody on the street. No cars passed.

I came to the bridge, to the driveway that descended from the street, ran along the pasture, the fallen fence, the two structures in the distance, the first large and hollow and somber, collapsing upon itself, and the second, visible at the edge of the stand of trees around the first, flickering dimly, a blue fluorescent light or TV on inside.

At the cottage I paused at the base of the steps leading up to the porch. There was a light on inside. The door was open. Music played, as before. A piano, I recall – something baroque. Not Bach – more playful than Bach – but measured, patient, lyrical. Couperin comes to mind.

I didn't go inside. I knew the way. I didn't want to disturb the woman, the caretaker, so I went around the house into the backyard, down the rough path toward the creek and Erin's hut.

The path ended at a small patio, a gazebo tangled overhead in flowerless wisteria. The girl's place was further on, down another path and beyond what could have been the gazebo's twin. This feature I did not remember from the time before, from my first visit:

two patios.

- I'm here.

It was Erin, her voice faint, flat in the darkness.

I continued down the path. There was no water in the creek but still I could feel the coolness of the sand in the bed, could smell something like the gurgling passage of water in the winter months.

Maybe there was water in the creek. In fact I didn't go close enough to see: I only assume, being July, that the creek was dry.

- What is it you see? she said.

I'd stopped before crossing the second patio. I was looking down the hill into the dark brambles on the bank of the creek. Had I heard something? Beyond the creek the land rose precipitously, a black screen of rock and pine, the ridge overhead marked by the opening of the vast starlit sky.

Through the round dark and empty window of her shed I saw nothing. An oval of darkness, like a mouth in surprise. But she was watching me, she saw me standing there.

Something about her voice, about her question caught my attention. Always eccentric, peculiar, this Erin Fines. *What is it you see?* So precise. What specific thing do you see? "What are you looking at?" or "What do you see?" would be off the mark, not of the world but the head, as if seeing were in doubt. But that was Erin, her odd way of speaking. Something old and formal, taunting, mocking in her voice. She'd seen it all before, the question implied – this paralyzed form, a head on a bed in a small room with one window and door: *What is it you see?*

I stood in the entrance to her room. I could make out the end of her bed, a whitegrey slope where her feet raised the sheet. Little else.

- It's nice having a friend like you, she said, who comes when he's called.

I looked back up the path, toward the cottage, a dim amber light burning inside now in silence.

- I don't remember the... I started to say of the second patio.

- Will you come in already, she said. I don't like talking to someone I can't see.

I stepped inside her room. I sat down in the chair on the left side of her bed, in the same place I'd sat before. She looked the same, exactly the same. Her cheeks, even in the darkness of the room, seemed flush.

- You don't remember what?

- You seem farther down, I said. From the house. Did she move your place?

Erin smiled, closed her eyes. Because she got tired of my *endless* demands, she said, this constant *dinging* of my little bell, wanting something, food, company, my back rubbed.

She held me in her gaze.

- No, you dolt, she said, it's the same path, the same gazebo. As last time. Nothing's changed.

- But there are two now.

- There've always been two.

She turned aside, reached across her body to the bedside table and lifted from a tray a glass of water, sipping it. The tray held a pitcher of water, another glass, and an empty ashtray. How on earth, she said, could *Nancy* move my place further from the house? Elongating the path and building a second gazebo two-thirds of the way down? On her own? In the time it's been since I last saw you?

- It's been a few years.

- It's been three years, she said. Anyways, don't be silly. Moving my place! Sometimes, Paul, she said, raising her voice, I wonder about you. About just how you get along.

The ashtray reminded me of my childhood, of my father, how he'd clean the various ashtrays about the house every night after we were in bed. In the morning they'd be clean enough to drink from. A terribly quiet man, in the morning I'd watch him from the upstairs window outside with the dogs, smoking, a cup of coffee in hand. It was a cold morning. He was wrapped up, the coffee steaming, his breath full of smoke and steam, a white frost covering the field. It was autumn. He'd rise early, make coffee, go outside with the dogs and smoke. He'd come in and with hardly a word enter his study and close the door. After a while I'd hear the typewriter clicking away, smell smoke through the door. I'd catch the bus for school and he'd still be in there, and when I came home in the afternoon he'd be gone, returning only after dinner, sitting by himself in silence at the table, eating, drinking, reading.

There was something else, too, in Erin's room, beyond the hint of smoke. A fragrance, a flower, *soap*. She'd been bathed.

- I call you and you come, she said. I suppose that makes you a friend. Isn't that what friends do?

And dogs, I thought. I really was a slavish fool when it came to girls.

- I'm glad you called, I said. I wanted to see you. How –

- I don't have many friends, she said. As you might have guessed.

- How did you know I was here?

She looked out of the window, up at the cottage. She shrugged, quietly said: I didn't. I just...

- But you sent the note.

- Did I? You know, Paul, she said, on our friendship, maybe it's the other way round. Maybe it's you who calls, and I'm the one who comes.

- What're you talking about?

- Please don't state the obvious, she said. Use your imagination, smart guy like you.

I felt small and condemned under her gaze. She turned so quickly, one moment a girl, the next something out of this world, timeless and far more powerful than anyone I knew.

And it was dark in her room. I could barely see her, not three feet from where I was sitting, under the sheet, upright at the head-board, watching me so carefully. But it wasn't her, her body, that is to say, that would take hold of you. It was a spirit, something in her, in the tone of her voice, in her presence. Touch and go, there and gone in an instant.

I wanted suddenly to press myself close to her body, to tuck myself into her arms, in affection but also in a kind of defense, to avoid her reach, her gaze.

She pressed her hands down into the mattress and lifted herself, shifting to the side, away from me.

- Come closer, if you'd like.

I was afraid of her. I wanted her, physically and mentally, en-tirely, I won't lie, but – but I couldn't act, do anything about this want. She was intimidating, a force of nature. She could read your thoughts. You have no contact with this person and she knows what you're doing, where you are, if you're in town visiting your aunt. How could she know that? Did George tell her? Did my aunt tell her? Certainly not. I'd made no plans on visiting. I called George one day and said I was coming down and he said that was fine. I left the next day. George was in Los Angeles, studying for his exams.

I stood up, turned and sat on the edge of the bed. I pushed my shoes off. I leaned back, feet up, my shoulder against hers. She put her hand on mine. Beneath the sheet I noticed the round edge of her lifeless leg. Slowly I reached out and touched it. I pressed my fingers against the hard appendage.

I hadn't noticed them before. The two books I'd lent her last time I was there, *The Woman Warrior* and *The Stand*, were on the table on her other side, by the ashtray.

- Did you like them?

- Yes. Thank you, she said quietly.

A breeze moved dry leaves in the gazebo outside. I waited for the black cat to make its appearance.

When she spoke I did not at first recognize her voice. Then I thought she was reading aloud. Then I realized she wasn't.

> My aunt haunts me – her ghost drawn to me because now, after fifty years of neglect, I alone devote pages of paper to her, though not origamied into houses and clothes. I do not think she always means me well. I am telling on her, and she was a spite suicide, drowning herself in the drinking water. The Chinese are always very frightened of the drowned one, whose weeping ghost, wet hair hanging and skin bloated, waits silently by the water to pull down a substitute.

- That sounds like *The Woman Warrior*, I said.

- It is. It's the end of the first chapter. I like this page very much. I liked most of the book very much.

- What did you like about it?

- About the book or this specific passage?

- The passage.

- I like the idea that the stories we tell keep certain characters alive. And that by proscribing other characters we can condemn them to punishments worse than death. That we can even continue to punish ghosts for the crimes they committed when they were alive.

- That's a terrible thing to do, don't you think?

- Maybe. That's beside the point. It's the power Kingston identifies in story-telling that I find appealing. To think I live in some sense in the stories you tell of me, or will tell of me – that excites me, I'm happy to say.

I laughed and said, I'm glad I could – bring some joy to your life.

- And vice versa, Paul, she said. The stories I will tell of you will maintain some aspect of your character, who you are, in the future. Imagine that, if you can, she said.

I waited for her to go on, my skin tingling.

She was quiet. I looked at the bed, at the shape of her legs beneath the sheet, at my legs next to this. Then I heard something peculiar. A crackle, a soft hiss. I turned, looked at her: she was looking at me, an enormous smile filling her face. Her teeth long and white, I caught me breath.

- Why did you read it? she said.

- You mean the –

- *The Woman Warrior*, she said.

- For school.

- You read things like that in school?

She hadn't finished high school. She would probably never go to college. She would probably never sit in a classroom or face a teacher ever again.

- We read all sorts of things in school.

- Even books by Stephen King?

- No, I said, smiling. That I read out of curiosity.

- Hmm.

- Hmm, what? What's that mean – *hmm?*

- That means I'm puzzled by what you choose to read out of a curiosity.

- And why's that?

- Seems rather timid, this curiosity of yours. I mean...

I waited again for her to go on. When she said nothing, I asked her to go on.

- If I could respond to my curiosities by choosing books to read, I don't think I'd pick up *The Stand*. That's what I mean.

- I see, I said. I understand.

- Do you?

- I think, yes. You're right. *The Stand* is not –

- If *that* is what you are curious about, Paul, I'd say you need to get out of your bedroom. Go outside. Take a walk in the woods. Go to the city, ride the subway. Go to a garage sale. Go to the zoo!

- I get it.

- Do you? I don't think you do, Paul. If your curiosity about things in the universe is reflected by the content of something like *The Stand*, then –

- I get it, Erin! I said, interrupting her the one and only time I can remember.

We sat in silence side by side.

- What did you make of it? I finally asked.

- It's a good story, she said. Too long. And the ending wasn't convincing.

- Endings can be difficult, I said.

- And how would you know?

I thought about that. I said: I guess I've read enough to get this sense – that the end of a story can come in many ways but only some of these really work.

She said nothing. Her chin dropped. She was staring at the bed in thought. She tucked in her elbow and grabbed the upper part of my arm, pulling. You can sit closer, she said. You won't hurt me.

I moved closer to her. My weight atop the bed pulled the sheet tight down against her legs.

- I like to feel the warmth of someone else, she said. Except for Nancy, I don't... I don't have much contact. After a moment she added: The body forgets. Even if I don't, my body does. It hardens, like a tree. The skin dies.

- Does she take you outside? I asked.

- Of course. Sometimes. But only at night. I think I mentioned that before. Days are... They can be hard... There's a telescope. It was my brother's.

- What do you look at?

- The moon. Planets. Galaxies far, far away.

- Where's your brother? I didn't know you had... Although something George had said came back to me suddenly: I'd made a mistake. I knew about the brother, he was –

She said nothing. I was flummoxed, speechless, wanting to apologize but not knowing exactly how, thinking too much about what to say, as young men do with young women.

- And so what about *your* curiosity? I finally asked, retreating, coming back to a point that puzzled me. If there's something in the world that you want to examine, do you turn to a book? Or go out into the yard at night?

When she didn't reply I leaned forward, looked into her face. She'd closed her eyes. I could see something moving under the pale skin of her face. She wasn't asleep. Was she thinking? Listening to something far off?

I'd said something wrong. I'd pushed her away with my questions. Her brother was dead.

- The only books I have are those people bring to me, she said. There is a small library up in the house, but most of those – four remain – I've read.

She laughed quietly and said, You might find it strange but Edgar Allan Poe is one of the few writers, of those available to me, I like to return to. I never tire of reading Poe.

- Poe's cool.

- And there's a poet – you've never heard of him – Robert Desnos, who is also very good. Comme tout est simple et étrange, she said, going on in French, which took me a moment to realize,

> Couchée sur le côté gauche,
> Je me désintéresse du paysage
> Et je ne pense qu'à des choses très vagues,
> Très vagues et très heureuses,
> Comme le regard las que l'on promène
> Par ce bel après-midi d'été
> À droite, à gauche,
> De-ci, de-là,
> Dans le délire de l'inutile.

- He died in a concentration camp in 1945.

After a moment she added,

- That last line is fun, *dans le délire de l'inutile*, which reminds me of you – in the delirium of uselessness. The French is prettier.

- So you think I'm delirious?

- I'm certain of it, Paul. And don't play games – you know it as well.

I smiled. She was right. She was always right. Though I wouldn't say I was useless, or felt useless.

- I did bring you those books, I said.

- True. You can be useful. If asked.

- How did you learn French?

- In school.

- In high school?

- What other school was there?

My hands were folded on my lap. She took the thin wrist of my right arm. Her skin was dry.

- I forgot.

- I know, she said.

She raised my arm, turning my hand palm up. She lifted my hand to her face and pressed her chin into the palm, my fingers against her cheek. She had the face of a child, smooth, soft. She lowered my hand, pressed the palm to her breast under her shirt, lifted my hand against her breast. She lowered my hand to her leg, lifted the sheet and pressed my fingers against the skin of her bare right leg. I felt the bone.

I said quietly, suddenly: I won't forget you.

- Yes you will, she said. Don't lie. You'll forget everything, she said. You'll never, ever be able to repeat the things I've told you. You'll try and you'll fail. And the harder you try, the more you'll fail. You'll come up with something, and it will sound right, or look right as you reflect on it, but in your heart you'll know that it's wrong.

I looked at her. Her bottom lip was full and red in the darkness, flushed as if she'd bitten down on it. Her leg was lifeless but there was an excess of life in her face, in her eyes. She was charged, animated.

My stomach tightened. My hand, still on her leg under the sheet, felt like it was holding a piece of wood. I could wrap my fingers around the limb. I tried to respond, to deny what she was saying, but the words caught in my throat.

I was frightened, again. The comfort I might have felt sitting beside her on her bed was an illusion. I was fooling myself. As I reflect now on the moment I realize it wasn't the first time she'd frightened me, I realize that the feeling of hopelessness and aphasia was more or less ongoing. It started as I came down the path to her room. The cottage at the top of the garden, where Nancy lived, was something ordinary and natural. Coming down the path, past the first gazebo and into and through the second gazebo, a replica of the first, however, you entered another world. There was a break somewhere. A sudden change of orientations: left became right, up down, positive negative. Everything looked the same in Erin Fines's world, you couldn't see the difference, but it was there.

It was a sense – I'm saying now, trying to put my finger on it – that she was not human in the way we are. She was dying, faster than us, certainly, but at the same time she wasn't. She was growing, not aging exactly, but moving incrementally toward... Becoming...

The stories I tell of you...

- What do you mean? I asked.

- You'll try, Paul. You'll fail.

- But I – I remember *some* things, Erin. How you just recited a French poem by memory, for example.

- Tell me the words.

My face was hot with shame. I couldn't speak French!

- In the delirium, the *dalir* of...

- Of?

- of uselessness.

- But the actual word was?

- Come on, Erin! Now you're...

- It's prettier in French. L'inutile, she said. But it doesn't matter. It's already happened, don't you see. So how can you tell me that you'll remember, that you'll remember any of this tomorrow?

- I will.

- That's bullshit, she said. You'll forget. You've already forgotten.

- But what are you asking for, for me to remember verbatim what you say? Nobody remembers conversations like that. You're not asking me to remember – you're asking me to record.

- No. That's different. That's cheating, letting a machine do the work you should do.

- Cheating! I'll remember that.

- Perhaps. Whatever. You still won't understand what it means.

Minutes later Carol found him outside. "I'm fine," he said. "I just needed some air."

She held him close, peered into his eyes. "You're okay? Something you aren't telling me?"

"Really, I'm fine. I was thinking of …"

"Of that silly article you're trying to write. Why break your neck over this? I mean – "

"I'm not. It's just – "

"Do it or don't. I don't see what the problem is."

He loved that about Carol. She was the most decisive person he'd ever known. Once she chose a course of action, she started immediately and followed through until finished.

He did not consider himself indecisive. For most things, there wasn't a problem.

Writing is different. He began to say something.

"Seems to me," she said, pulling him along, they were returning inside, "you don't want to write this piece for your old friend. So don't do it. Go home, respond to her query. Tell her thanks but you can't help. Done. You can do it from my place. And get on with your life."

"I think I'll finish what I've started."

They sat down. The orchestra had left the stage. The quintet, Dylan in the center, Jennifer on the right, had taken its place. She wore a black dress. With the cello between her knees, the dress rose up her ankles. Sockless feet in small black pumps, he found himself, even at a distance, entranced by her pale skin, the inside of her leg. He tried to remember the last time he'd seen the inside of Carol's legs.

The music began suddenly. His thoughts were elsewhere. He might have seen the musicians lift their instruments, take a breath, and start, but his mind didn't recognize these movements.

But then it was there, the melody. The grounded strings, walk-ing, carefree, and the clarinet, like a bird rising from the earth, seek-ing a limb, looking down at the visitors in the woods, guiding them into the shadows.

He'd heard the piece before. He was... It was... In Ithaca, New York. He was in his late twenties. It was a gallery. He was a janitor. He worked nights, usually between nine and midnight. If there was a show, or a concert, he helped set the stage, the lights, the seating.

The night he heard the Brahms quintet, he took a seat near the back. Next to him sat a Russian fellow and his English wife. He was a painter. Studying painting, anyways. They met from time to time to talk about books, play chess, listen to music. The Russian – he called him David, though that wasn't his name – was conceited, friendly but full of himself. A sore loser at chess. His wife, Emily, told him that if David lost, he talked about the game for days after-ward, bothered, sulking, wanting a rematch.

Paul and Emily met for coffee. They went to the movies, he seemed to recall, a couple times, the two of them alone, when David had work to finish.

David drew Paul. Large, black and white images. There he was, his naked seated form, tacked up on the wall of David's studio.

Hearing Brahms, that's what he remembered. *It's a walk down a path, into the woods.* Having dinner with David and Emily, his image on the wall in the other room, watching Emily across the table, undressing her in his mind's eye as he coiled spaghetti onto his fork, leaned down, shoved it into his mouth.

Nobody takes walks in the woods any more.

Where are those drawings now? David's work?

After the concert, Carol stepped aside to talk with some people she knew. Vogel, outside, found Dylan smoking in an alcove. He was talking to someone elsewhere, soft blue light flickering in his eye, a projection only he could see.

"That was beautiful."

The boy looked up, momentarily dazed, blind, found Paul in the shadow. He said: "Excuse me. Pardon me." He said to Paul: "Look at this."

In the darkness Dylan ran his thumb across his anlis. A flicker of light and then Paul could see what Dylan saw. It was the performance, the quintet. The point of view was close, among the musicians.

"Listen," Dylan said.

He listened. It was a passage near the end of the piece, before the coda. The syncopation between the clarinet and the violin was complex, executed perfectly to Paul's ear.

"Hear that?" Dylan said.

"Hear what? It's lovely. Sounds right to me."

Dylan paused the recording, rewound, started again. "Listen." Once again, he listened. He'd close his eyes to hear better, but it wouldn't do anything: the image was inside.

"Is there something wrong?" Paul said.

Dylan, his face deep in shadow, his eyes flickering blue, angry, said: "We didn't play it like that. I was behind, off by half a beat.

127

I'm sure of it. It's the sort of thing… Ask John."

John was the violinist.

"I don't understand," Paul said.

"It's corrected."

"Corrected? Who corrected it? Who made the recording?"

"That's just it. I did. It's my camera. I haven't shared this any-one."

"But others recorded it. Is it possible that…"

Vogel didn't know what to say. The tech was beyond his ken.

"… That another recording, nearly exact to the one I made, was corrected and then doubled over mine? Is that what you're…"

It was an idea. Not his, but one. "Can they do that?"

Dylan was quiet for a moment, watching, listening. Finally he said, "There've been other clues." He touched his anlis, closed his eyes. The image disappeared. Then it was the two of them standing in a dark alcove. Far off the burble of people talking, laughter.

"They call it enemesen," Dylan said.

"En em es en," Vogel repeated slowly.

"The letters. N M S N. There are two. One – "

"Two what?"

"Viruses." Dylan looked up. He spoke quietly, lower than usual.

"Viruses? For the … computer?"

Dylan smiled. Nobody used that word anymore. "It's in the net-work," he said, a glance up. "One, I was saying, frees up memory. It accesses memory, finding or creating memory where there was none."

"Memory?"

"One result of this is that everything appears to speed up. That, and things like this – changes, differences, corrections. You know it was one way, but the genius, making connections, returns it to you another. The way it should be. The way everyone wants it to be."

"I'm not sure I follow."

Dylan paused. Would he explain? He knew Paul well enough not to try.

"It's not memory, in the sense of storage. In this form it's only access, space, the freedom to shuffle and resort everything, inventing."

Vogel thought about it. He drew a blank. He said: "And the other? The second?"

"The opposite. Anenemesen."

"Loss of memory?"

"Yes. Sort of. Right. Space reduced. Memory acts as if full. Acts as if it is trying to remember everything."

Vogel's thoughts drifted suddenly. It was the photograph he'd seen a day or two ago, of Stoikov, in the library. There was a man beside her, a man who was not there, not supposed to be there. He was sure of it.

A correction? Invention?

"Things slow down, in this case," Dylan said. "Frequent errors occur."

"Errors?"

"Misinformation, mixed results. Data dumps. You find things in the wrong place. In the wrong time."

Joel was his name. Joel Vander... Vender?

"Eventually she stops, freezing up. Lights on, nobody home, as they say," Dylan said, smiling.

"She?"

He held out his anlis, small black button in his hand.

"She's remembered everything – or thinks she has – but remembers nothing."

"You are talking about... I forget the name..."

Dylan nodded. "*Feihung,*" he said, closing his hand.

"And what you're saying, then, of this recording is that…"

"I'd say it's the one, the first, freeing up, synthesizing, presenting what never was, but what it thinks we would like to see and hear."

"And this is bad?"

The young man frowned. Shook his head quickly, as if shooing a fly. He leaned forward, bending, Paul felt, for his height. "Are you crazy?" he said. "You're joking, right?"

"I…"

"Of course it's bad. It's fucking awful. When she starts to… Make shit up? Tell you about things going on that are not real? Tell you about things *in your life* that are not real?"

Dylan waited. Paul was silent, processing.

Dylan said: "Yes, Paul, it is bad. This is bad. Whichever way it turns, the one or the other – which, they're saying, was supposed to be an antidote to the first – NMSN is going to stop everything. Lights out."

"And there's no cure?"

Dylan snorted, shook his head. He moved suddenly, reaching into his coat pocket. He came out with a pack of cigarettes. He shook one out, bent down, lit up.

"I didn't know you smoked."

"Sometimes," he said. "And no. There is no cure. Not yet. Maybe they'll get it. Maybe they won't. Anyways," he said, inhaling, smiling, smoke rising from his nostrils and mouth, "you don't have to worry. It's such a small thing, for now, the odds of picking it up are slim."

"But you think you might have it."

If he has it, Paul, then…

Lucy and Feihung were synced, the image stream seamless.

"Even if I do. It's not clear yet how it moves. At least I haven't heard anything on this. It's networked, not local."

A figure came around the corner, stopped, caught her breath.

"There you are," she said. Jenny, cellist. "I've been looking all over for you."

Dylan stepped away. "See you later?" he asked over his shoulder.

"Not sure. I was thinking of heading back. Finishing some work."

"Hi, Paul," Jenny said with a smile, slow, it would seem, on recognition. There was some light on the balcony, around the edge of the structure. Paul remained in the shadow. "You mean that thing you're writing," she said.

Paul smiled. "Yes. That thing."

"I think that's wonderful," Jenny said, her tone unreadable, young and precocious, "contributing to this lady's book. Helping her like that, for posterity."

Vogel didn't know how to respond. The girl could've been speaking Greek. "Dylan," he said, "let's talk soon. I'd like to hear more about this… I think I might have…"

"What's that?" Jenny said, pulling Dylan in close. The tall, handsome young man, his eyes on Paul. He'd let her go. It wouldn't be long now. She wanted him more than he wanted her. "What was it? … What were you two…" Clawing for his attention.

The boy and girl walked away.

Vogel looked on the dark, ruinous city. Skyscrapers downtown, towering shadows in the murk, the lonesome flicker of light. The sky was heavy, stacked with clouds. Rain was coming. He could smell it.

"Lucy?"

>> I'm here. <<

"Was all that true? What Dylan said."

>> Enemesen is a virus. <<

"And it does what he says it does?"

>> I'm not sure I can answer that. <<

Vogel smiled to himself. He felt closer to Lucy more and more every day.

"Not sure because you don't know or not sure because you're reluctant to."

Lucy paused for longer than usual. Then she said: >> Both.<<

Vogel took a breath, sighed, stepped out of the dark. "When you're ready to talk," he said, "I'm here for you."

>> I know, Paul. <<

NMSN or not, Vogel enjoyed the performance very much. He remembered, in his youth, practicing and practicing, feeling like such a small part in the larger system. For the longest time, the music sounded broken, like nothing. Fragments. But then, coming together as a group, on the stage, the tapestry was complete. Everything in its place, the story worked.

The voices, the parts, the instruments, their harmony was at once instantaneous and epic, reaching back through time, over countless performances to the original, to the composer, to the room in which he imagined the piece, writing, note by note.

The performance is one of a kind, and one of many. It could be the first performance, the very first. (For some, Vogel thought, remembering the two boys, dressed up, eager for the music to begin, it was.) At the same time, the music lives in a history of performances. Singular and plural, music pulls us in these contrary directions. All of the performances, of the Brahms quintet, say, from eighteen-ninety to the present, come together in each performance.

The composer is present, here with us, in the music. That is his voice, those are his ideas being expressed for the first time.

Tomorrow it will be something else. The recordings. All the recordings. The recording in Dylan's head, his recalling the mistake. The missed beat. Nobody heard it – except Dylan and John. Nobody will remember it. In time even Dylan will have forgotten.

Especially if the recordings do his remembering for him.

The hardest part of performing, he recalled, was the end, afterwards. He never cared that much for performing. He was always nervous, sick with nerves every time he started. At the same time, walking away was pure misery. The spirit is spent. The aftermath – cold, hollowed out inside. All of that work, that concentration, listening, playing over and over again – it's all gone up like smoke. You've built something for an instant, for the satisfaction of this audience, who know nothing, and now it's gone, behind us.

Why didn't I bring a tape recorder? I should have known. I knew what I was getting into, going up there that night.

"No you didn't. You didn't know what to expect. You couldn't have known."

"Of course I could. I knew from the first time, the second time, that is, I met her, sitting with her. I knew about her accident, the peculiar…"

"You can't even say it. You don't even know what it was."

"She had a perfect memory."

"What's that even mean?" Lucy made a sound like laughter. "And you think that if you had known what to expect before going up to meet Erin Fines that second time, you would have taken with you a… What did they have then? Tape? A tape recorder, is that what you said?"

He couldn't remember. Did they still use tape then? Or did they have digital devices? Tape came to mind, seemed right. He could see the tiny cassette in his mind.

"Yes," he said.

She made the sound again. "You are lying to yourself, Paul. She was right. You tell yourself these little lies about your past in order to sleep at night."

"I'm going to shut you off."

"Go ahead!"

He didn't. She was playing with him. Sometimes he enjoyed the company, her attempts at humor. He enjoyed witnessing her progress. She was like a child. He tried to remember Silvia as a child. It was hard. In time that period was closer to him than his meeting with Erin Fines, but for some reason the details were vague. He'd decided at some point to let those memories go.

Was there a similarity between the growth of a child and the growth of Lucy? Surely the programmers had this metaphor in mind when they designed her.

And there it is again. *Metaphor*. It even sounds sinister. A sphinx. You bend backwards at her word. Crushing difference, willfully pretending, closing your eyes, that these two things could be the same. They aren't. They weren't. They'd never be. But the metaphor, working its magic both ways, begins to warp our understanding. We treat them as if they were like us.

"She was quiet for a time after that," he wrote. "I must have dozed off."

שׁ

I remember waking to the sound of her voice. She was saying something about insects, how she could hear them walking in the grass, creeping in the walls, in the ceiling above. Termites, she thought, eating the wooden skeleton inside the adobe structure, hollowing it out. She couldn't help but envision the natural end to the process in three to four years.

She then recalled without pause the first time she saw the structure. It was a small, cubic building at the bottom of the garden, a covered patio at its entrance. There was a window cut in the shape of a circle right of the entry. It is a large window with a thick sill: one could sit in the window. Like the doorway, I recall it always being open. I do not recall seeing glass in this window, only the opening, a large dark hole.

Behind the structure – through the wall above her head, as she slept – the yard came to a sudden end, the earth falling down into a creekbed. The creek ran from mid-winter through the spring. Several times it had flooded, the water rising to within inches of the base of the structure, which had originally been a tool shed.

She could see it, then, as she'd first looked upon it. She was seven years old. It was the afternoon of August 10th, 1988. Her parents were in the house preparing a late lunch. There was a large maroon truck in the yard before the house. Movers were carrying in boxes, stacking them in the empty living room. She recalled passing directly through the house, which she'd never seen before, front door to back, passing the cottage, dark and cold in the shadow of the mountain, and following a narrow path into a field of thistles, brambles, blackberry vines. There was an orchard of plum and apple trees, weeds up to the low black branches, everything overgrown without care. The structure beyond the orchard, practically buried in thistles and vines, stood solemn and neglected, a pile of rock washed down the mountain in the last ice age.

She could see it the following day as well, when she came down to it and, shoving a dozen wooden crates up against one wall and sweeping the floor, she made it her own. It would be hers, first as a hideout, later, much later as a bedroom.

And she could see it the following day and the day after that and the day after that. The structure, every moment of its existence as far as she was concerned – from that August afternoon in '88 – lived in her memory, in her mind's eye. Once or twice she tried to go further, since it predated her arrival: built in 1934, shortly after the house was completed, she had fifty-four years to imagine, the sun rising and falling over its curious rooftop some nineteen thousand times.

She could hear insects in the walls destroying the place. And yet, they couldn't, they wouldn't, because it was there in her mind, every time she closed her eyes, over and over again, impervious.

The world for her, I realized, existed in this plural condition, in an eternal instant of identification between image and object.

She would reconstruct days from her childhood. Nancy would sit with her through the night as Erin held forth, describing what happened from the moment she woke – on a Thursday in the fall of 1991, say – to the moment, eighteen hours later, she went back to sleep. To her listener, the description would exceed perfection, detailed in high definition before there was such a thing. A perfect simulation.

The perfect reconstruction, however, she said, could not expose the materials of the construct in the present. She could not say, for example: "I can make the day." "Let me describe for you…" To acknowledge the act would undermine the simulation. The difference, then, between one and the other was this introduction, the edge of a frame, so to speak, which gave away the second as a reconstruction and not the real thing.

On the other hand – I recall thinking or feeling – the difference between the one day and the other might not be a difference at all. The introduction, as I'm calling it, might be hardwired into every construction. What is a day, if not a series of events that follows from an answer to this question, or statement, "Here we are again. Another day…"?

The singular experience – the individual, the instance – cannot be severed from a generalization. We hold a single day up against the day before, against a week, a year, a lifetime of experiences.

"Go back to that metaphor of the frame," he said, talking aloud again. "If memory transfers this sense of difference – that a so-called real day is not like a remembered day because the remembered day is somehow marked as a memory – carrying it along as part of the package, the memory itself, then how can we tell what's a process of memory alone and what's original? Maybe the frame is always there, as we wake in the morning and fall asleep at night."

"I'm not sure I follow."

"We don't see it, of course. But we feel it. The day is only a day because it looks and sounds like other days. We don't consciously make this calculation, but it's there. The mind works behind a curtain."

"Okay."

"But if that's the case, then perhaps memory leaves all sorts of fingerprints on the things it brings forth. And we immediately assume that they are aspects of the original. We assume, as well, that memory transfers the past to the present, to the future, with integrity, with disinterest in the object it carries. But who's to say memory doesn't have its favorites? Preferences. Who's to say that memory doesn't dwell and linger in one room longer than another? That when we ask it to fetch something for us that it doesn't care for, who can say what it really does, going to fetch this thing, bringing it begrudgingly back? Spit in the soup, you know."

"The soup," Lucy said, slowing down, "being the remembered scene, the memory."

"A quick study, you."

"But what's the spit?"

ש

Her comment about curiosity was nagging at me.

- So you think I should go to the zoo more?

- That's not what I meant.

- Erin, excuse me but how can you – how would you know – tell me to get out of my bedroom if I'm curious about what's happening in the world? That doesn't strike you as an odd thing to say?

- No. It doesn't.

- As if you would know.

We'd slid down onto the bed, hardly sitting up at that point, facing the ceiling, shoulder to shoulder, our faces just inches apart. She looked at me in the dark.

- Oh, because I can't leave my room, that's what you're saying, she said. Great observation, Sherlock. First place for observation goes to Paul Vogel everyone.

- You disagree?

- First, the notion that because I can't do something means I can't advise you to do it is ridiculous. Equally absurd is the idea that we can't know or understanding something unless we experience it first-hand. Bunk, Paul.

- That's not what I was saying.

- Yes it is. I'd say most of what we know and understand about the universe we speak of without first-hand experience. Second, I wasn't attacking your choice of books or manner or degree of curiosity. If Stephen King is a target of your curiosity, fine. I don't care. What I was getting at was the insincerity of your claim. You admitted that you were wrong to say King answered your curiosity, or that you'd chose to read *The Stand* out of curiosity. Didn't you?

- Did I?

- You said *I see, I understand, I get it, I get it.* Well, excuse me,

Paul, but you don't get it. You still don't get it. Because if you did you wouldn't say something as stupid as what you just said – *So you think I should go to the zoo more?* You did not mean *curiosity* when you said you read King out of curiosity. *That's* what I was getting at. You did not read King's book out of curiosity. But that's what you said –

- How...

I caught myself. I was losing the argument. I'd already lost.

She was silent. I heard her tongue rub her teeth, her lower lip.

- Chit-chat like that, she said, lowering her voice as if sharing a secret, when you say things that you don't mean, really bothers me, Paul. Don't do it. Especially don't do it with me. If I could –

She coughed. Sitting upright suddenly, falling away from me, she covered her mouth with her hand and coughed hard for a few seconds. Then she sat without moving, on her elbow, her back to me.

- I'm okay, she said.

I put my hand on her shoulder. She pulled away.

Paraplegics sometimes develop breathing problems. Being bedridden, the immobility, is hard on the lungs. Muscles in the abdomen atrophy. I learned that much later, after '29, when there was a lot of immobility.

- I know I shouldn't smoke, she said, but I do. I'm hurting myself. Why?

She lay back and swallowed.

- My excuse, she said, is that...

I waited for her to finish. She didn't. She shifted her weight, took my left hand firmly in hers, said quietly: Tell me about your travels.

"What did she see in me? Why did she ask for me, that first time, in 2001, to bring her those books? She didn't even... I was just..."

Nothing was particular, just a thing in itself for her. Everything was connected, a latticework of causes, other conditions, other states of being. Like Heraclitus, she saw the world as a constant metamorphosis of substance from one state into another. Moreover, she could not separate sensation from observation or understanding. Every image she described to me was also a description of some kind of physical exertion, a kind of concentration, using the eye in a particular way, breathing in a particular way, thinking in a particular way. And so on. And the sheer complexity of these descriptions – of seeing her cat, Pluto, for example, come into the room – suggested that she was failing, *failing*, in fact, at abstract thought, at formalizing sense data. We sometimes kid ourselves about living in the present, gathering rose buds while ye may. But that's all she had, the present, completely attuned to, captivated and imprisoned by, each instant.

"Her memory," he said, "unlike ours, unlike human memory, excluded repetition or restoration. Her memory, rather, described the capacity of her attention to the world, the direction of her vacuuming gaze, described a kind of storage space wherein everything present existed *sui generis*, temporarily in itself in its metamorphosis."

She told me about days in her childhood. I'd have to stop her at some point, to ask a question, to adjust the aim of her narrative. Otherwise we'd be there all night following the steps of eight year old Erin through a day in her life.

"You brought from – " he said, trying to remember. "The man I mêt, Lucy, in the station. It was something he said. *By your will, you brought from nothing, everything*. Do you know that?"

"Do I know that the man you met in the station said these words to you, or do I know this expression?"

"I've heard it before. Where's it from?"

"In *Revelation*," Lucy said, "there is a similar line." She began to recite and analyze. He was only half listening.

What would happen to the day it took her to describe a day? Was it something lost, or could she reconstruct that day as well?

The reconstruction would include a small, the smallest, subtlest, difference. Namely, a frame, the present surrounding the narration of the past. "On the morning of August tenth, nineteen eighty-eight, I – "

The perfect reconstruction, the perfect simulation, however, would not expose the materials of the construct in the present. They would be hidden. Words behind the words. No exposition, no "On the morning of." Rather, the day would simply begin.

You brought from nothing everything.

He took a taxi home. Carol invited him over. He insisted on going home. "I'd like to finish this thing."

Instead of turning left and entering his building, he continued walking down the quiet street. It was not a conscious decision, passing his building, going for a walk. It just came upon him. When he realized this he found the possibilities amusing, that something could just "come upon him" like that.

The sky was dark and still. The rain had stopped. The canopy overhead hung motionless, like dark blue and green paper cutouts, not trees.

He walked down Market. He thought about Dylan, about the future, about this computer virus the boy had mentioned. None of it made sense to him. Not the possibility of the virus – he didn't think Dylan was making that up – but the mechanics of the virus itself. *Finding space, taking space, making space* – were they all the same, for the machine? *Creating memory where there was none. Virtual memory in a virtual dimension.* It didn't make any sense.

When he thought about his present, his state of being as a man of sixty-one, it didn't make much sense. It never had. The present never made sense. The past – sometimes. Like shuffling square plates around a puzzle, trying to connect the dots, the lines, make the picture. You knew it could come together in the correct order – the picture *was* there. It just took patience, practice.

But the present? You might move some pieces, begin to bring the picture forth, only to discover a thousand more pieces on the margin that you didn't see before. It's not a house that you thought you were constructing, but a city. Not a city but a megalopolis.

>> What *are* you doing? <<

He descended at Montgomery Station.

>> Where do you think you're going? The station is closed.<<

"I want to check something."

>> Stop. Turn around. Come home. <<

"Quiet, you. I just want to – "

>> Paul? Paul. *Paul.* You *know* – <<

With a touch of his thumb, he shut her off.

The iron gate at the bottom of the steps was locked. Darkness in the vast interior, under the street.

He thought for a moment that his meeting a few days before – *When was that?* – with the man in the station was a dream, something made up perhaps in his reflecting on Stoikov and George and a certain librarian, a friend of his from those years, and Erin. Maybe it had happened years before, when the station was opened.

No. It had been two, three days ago. After work. He was sure of it. That was the day Stoikov contacted him.

He looked through the iron bars of the gate. It was quiet inside the station. He thought he could hear water running. He peered into the darkness until a chill came over him. Then he turned and climbed the wet steps back to the street.

>> I told you. The station is closed. I'll send a cab. <<

"Don't. I'll walk. I like to walk sometimes."

But then too he didn't head home. He continued down Market. There was nobody else out – not a single person nor vehicle on the street. Further down, near the clock tower, he heard a commotion in the trees, birds, cats, nocturnal creatures making a ruckus. The Embarcadero was dark, quiet. Water clicked gently at the curb, the vast and inky black of the bay.

He started around the block, without realizing it, toward Ecker. "The scene of the crime," he thought as turned down a dim and vacant sidewalk.

He was looking up for a street name, passing an alley, when a man said: "I know you?"

Vogel was startled but not frightened. It was the man he was looking for.

"No," he said.

The man was tall, in a heavy and filthy parka, the hood up around his head, his dark face. Despite the warmth of the night, the man wore what looked to be a wool hat, a scarf. He had on gloves, heavy boots. His jacket and clothing were all the same color, in the dim light an oily dark brown, color of clay soil.

Vogel glanced at the face looking down at him. Something compelled him to keep his eyes down, away from this other's gaze. It was not just heavy clothing: the man was enormous.

"Domingo send you?"

"No. Nobody sent me. I'm the man – "

"That fella," the man said. "Knew I knew you from somewhere."

The man had a large black plastic bag, full as Santa Claus, in his hand, at his heels. At his feet lay another bag, this one canvas.

"What you want?"

>> What *are* you doing, Paul? <<

"Nothing," he said. "I was out for a walk. And…"

The man stared at him, the whites of his eyes flickering wet in the dark face.

"I went by the station," Vogel said. He didn't know how to continue. Could he tell the man that he was looking for him, that he wanted to talk? About what?

He might as well be looking for a bear in the woods, he realized. Talking to animals. This world we live in.

The man grunted. He took a breath, twisted his hand quickly around the stretched top of the plastic bag, lifted it, its contents clattering tightly together. The man started to turn, entering the alley. He said: "Make yourself useful. Give us a hand. Take that will you?" He gestured at the bag on the ground as he walked away.

>> Don't touch it, Paul. I'll call the police. Would you like me to call the police? <<

"The police?" he said quietly.

The man, shuffling into the dark, paused, glanced back, sighed deeply. "Coming or not? I've things to do."

"One sec," Vogel said. Looking away, to Lucy he whispered, "I want you to be quiet for a few minutes. I'll shut you off if you say another word."

>> I'll turn myself on. <<

"I'll pop the battery, you stubborn bitch. Now bug off. Give me a few minutes. I want to talk with this man."

>> I'm calling the police. <<

"To tell them what, exactly? I can't help a man who asks for help?"

>> He's a criminal. Helping him makes you a criminal. <<

"He is not a… Give me ten minutes. I'll come home in ten minutes."

>> Starting now. The clock is running. <<

Paul Vogel turned back, faced the man.

"Finished?" the man said. He stood motionless in the alley, watching.

Vogel took the bag. It was heavy, solid. He hadn't lifted anything with one hand so heavy in a long time. It felt good.

"Your mother?" the man said.

Vogel chuckled. "Might as well be."

"The machine, then."

Vogel didn't respond. He took the canvas bag and followed the man down the alley.

They stopped at a pair of black metal doors. Small white stenciled words, illegible after years of exposure, city grime and graffiti, announced what the entry was originally for. The man rifled in his coat pocket, came up with a small ring of long necked keys. He lifted these close to his face, dropping them one by one along the curve of the ring. Then finding what he wanted he slid the key into a tiny hole high up on the door, turned, pulled. The door opened in silence.

The man jerked a shoulder. "Go. Watch your step."

Vogel entered with the bag. Stairs down on his right, a dim light far below.

"Go on," the man said at his back.

He took a step down. Then another. He expected to hear Lucy squawking in his ear, but she was silent.

Descending he heard the man lock the door behind them and then follow. The bottom of the staircase opened onto a hallway, lit above by small round fluorescent bulbs, lights the size of marbles, ten of them in a line, burning fluently in yellow and blue waves if you stared too long.

A vein of Montgomery Station, Vogel guessed. No man's land.

There was a door at the end of the hall. "Push. Should be open," the man said at his back.

Then the space opened up, the dim light of the hall casting an arc over the floor of the station, a chamber he vaguely remembered passing through years before. On his left, a football field away, a soft rectangle of blue light: the gate, stairs up.

Once again the man turned, closed the door they passed through and locked it. Now the darkness was nearly total. His eyes adjusted. He could make out the bulk of the man before him. It moved away shuffling along the wall. He followed. He kept his right hand against the wall, cold cement, periodic breaks, lines cut in the tiles, his eyes peeled on the figure before him. After a minute, they turned right into another hall.

"Stay close!" the man barked. "Tracks to the left there, down that edge."

But Vogel could see nothing of an edge or tracks.

When the man stopped Vogel nearly walked right into him. The smell caught him: sharp, of urine, smoke, gasoline, a body unwashed, the stench of a man apart from things for a long time.

The man ran his fingertips over the wall, quickly rubbing, stopping at a point, finger down, keys came clattering out, the door pushed open, a tall slab of haunted darkness before him. The man stepped forward and vanished. "Wait. Don't move." He shuffled about the dark. He set down his burden. The soft sound of his tapping, stumbling, lifting, sorting through various things. Then the grind and spark, spark and flare of a lighter. A leaf of white flame rose in the darkness. The man lit a candle. He reached out, lit another, a third. Vogel entered. The room felt different – small, safe, ordered. There was a long cluttered table, shelves along one wall, what looked like a bench, a large sunken chair.

Gently he closed the door.

"Sit. I'll get a drink."

Paul looked at the chair, smelled it at a distance, took the wooden bench, dragging it away from the table. Save for a small space at one end, the table was a dark inscrutable mess, a creature-like heap, the jetsam of everyday life. Aluminum cans, jars, papers of all sorts, a pen and pencil, a pile of black nuts and bolts, a basket of redbrown apples, apple cores, PVC piping, several lengths of steel pipe, a tangled ball of wiring, a bird's nest, tools, a green bushy wreath, an open toolbox, several cans of paint, a paintbrush hardened black, what looked like a stack of white dishes, sea shells and fishbones, shavings wooden and metallic coiled in their dust, paperback books in towers of various heights, a camera, a pile of pictureless frames, a WWF calendar from decades back, panda cuddling its young, some glass bottles, a lusterless MacBook, a tabletop microscope, glimmering DVDs, a vice, what looked like a gun.

"Is that a gun?"

The man set a tin cup on the table. He turned, bent down, reached into a cupboard low against the wall, came up with a bottle, twisting the top off. A dark liquid poured forth. The man lifted the cup cranelike with his large fingers and lowered it before Vogel.

"What's that?"

"Wine. Friend's vintage. Up north."

The man stood over the table, his large hand still wrapped about the neck of the bottle. He was waiting.

Vogel sipped the drink. Wine, sure enough.

The man grunted. "Not bad. What you say?"

Mouthful of cotton. The grape was heavy, far back. "Delicious," Vogel said. "Thank you."

"Don't mention it," the man said. "Don't get much company."

The man poured himself a cup. He drank. He said: "It's a gun.

Antique now. A sig-sauer em-eighteen. Service weapon."

"You were in the…"

The man grunted. Vogel could hear him breathing through his nose.

The man stepped about the room, cup in hand, poking through his collection of odds and ends. He set the cup down, took off his jacket, a dark flannel shirt underneath, suspenders holding up pants large enough for two Paul Vogels.

"Doesn't work, I don't think… Syria," the man said. "Two tours." The man took a loud deep breath, head down. He turned, stepped into a dark adjacent room. There he lit another candle.

Vogel stood, stepped toward the other room.

Rooms, he saw. The first presented a curious array: in the candle light, nothing was clear, but on one wall, filling it entirely, he thought he saw something like a fuse box, only it was an enormous matrix, row upon row of fuses, sockets.

His host passed through the room, hunkering down through a small opening in the opposite wall.

Vogel stepped into the room. Two opposing walls were covered in what looked like light sockets, some filled with dark glass bulbs, others open, skullish eyes. There was a mattress on the floor to the left, a heap of blankets piled at one end.

Dim light arose in the next room. It was a larger space, lit along one wall with the small bulbs he'd seen before, entering.

On a table in the center of the room, a wide and flat structure. On closer inspection: thousands of plastic bottles, stacked and arrayed and fastened together.

"Some juice in this panel," the man said, raising his chin at the wall, the lights. "I can run it to the other room on an extension when I want it."

"So you live here?"

The man grunted. "Call it that."

The man had a deep voice. He spoke slowly, groaning, grunting, breathing hard, clearing his throat. He was bearded, black, so filthy Vogel thought he saw layers of dirt on his cheeks, forehead. No telling, actually, what color the man originally was.

"What's that?" Vogel asked about the structure on the table.

"My boat," the man said.

"You're making a boat?"

The man grunted, took a breath. Hands on his craft, chin down, he said into his beard, "That's what I said."

"For?"

The man looked directly at him.

"The flood." The whites of the man's eyes flickered under his hood.

"Meaning?"

The man raised a hand, stepped toward his guest, pointed at the cup he'd carried with him, "Drink up," pushed him without pushing back through the circuit breaker into what was the living room.

"You think there'll be a flood?" Vogel said, returning to the bench.

The man grunted, almost laughed. "Think? No. It's certain. As certain as the wine you drink." He poured himself another cup. "Happening already."

"The flood?"

He grunted. "Are you blind, friend?"

The tunnel was closed. Trains hadn't run in almost a year. Down the peninsula they still ran, he'd heard, but here at the bay, nothing. Nothing for a while. What was, had been, the heart of the city, was now still. The streets empty, wooded. Scattered lights on above, in buildings like his, but down below, outside, a peaceful resolve. The embarcadero as he'd known it years before was gone, under the surf. The old clock tower, a pylon, memorial to that other time.

The transformation came slowly. It was something, like the damaged tunnel, that elicited a response from the city. There was a plan. There were plans. It wasn't a flood properly speaking, not in his view. "I'm aware of the water," Vogel said. "I just…"

The man nodded. "Like all the rest," he said. "But it'll be here sooner than you think. It's coming now, running now, rising. You can hear it if you listen."

The man closed his eyes, groaned softly. "You haven't seen nothin," he said. "A sprinkle. Morning dew compared to what's coming."

Vogel finished his cup of wine, set the cup on the table.

In the candle light, the underground man looked tall and formidable. There was something animal, bearish and rodent, about the man, and his dwelling something of a burrow.

"You from around here?" Vogel said, hardly listening.

The man looked at him. He looked aside, at the large plastic bag he'd carried down from the street. He lifted it, brought it to the workshop, the raft. Vogel didn't see the contents of the bag but realized suddenly that it probably contained plastic of various types and forms.

Vogel looked at the canvas bag he'd brought down. That wasn't plastic inside.

The man returned. "Lived here all my life. Cept for those years in the army – here, San Fran." The man sat down in the chair. He reached back, lifted the bottle of wine, poured himself another cup. He held out the bottle to Vogel's extended arm, cup. Poured. The man's bearded face shifted, stretched, smiling a mouthful of rotten teeth. "Listen," he said. "Hated every goddamn minute of it – the army – godless war… But, you know, the world then, even war, it

151

was better, a better place, than what we have now."

"Better than living in a subway, you mean."

The man grunted. "Not at all. Better than living anywhere. We lost a beautiful thing when the planet died."

Now Vogel smiled. He was warming up to this odd situation, this man in his burrow. "I wouldn't say the planet's dead."

The man grunted, loudly cleared his throat. "Are you blind!? Look around you. City's dead. State, dead. Country, dead... The sea – even the sea – dead. The sky... When was the last time you saw the sky, friend?" The man closed his eyes, settled back, down into his old chair. Quietly he said, "You live up there in the towers, electronic bubble. You don't see what's happening. Don't see because – because you have lost the ability to look for yourself – with your integrated... – and now, now that I ask you to look around, you, like a child, don't know how."

"I know how to – "

"In a bubble, friend! You see nothing. Sure, you move your eyes. You move your head. All gestures, like a puppet. But it doesn't mean you see, doesn't mean you know what you're looking at. Because it's coming. I tell you. Hear me. The eyes of the blind will open – the ears of the deaf be unsealed." The man caught his breath, lowered his face in thought, memory. "Water – will run – in the wasteland. The *asphodel* will burst into flower and rejoice and sing for joy."

Vogel drank. For a home brew, it was passable wine. Better than passable – it was quite good.

Asphodels, he thought. *Flower of the dead*, he recalled, not knowing the source.

"That scripture?" he said.

The man grunted, glared at his guest. "Like all the rest. You mock me."

"No. I just don't believe you."

The man cleared his throat, raised his large empty hands, opened and closed them several times quickly, stretching. It was not cold in this underground dwelling. It was surprisingly comfortable, warmer than the breezy street above, but the man was still dressed as if for late fall.

No fall. No winter. An endless spring. Paradise.

"Belief has nothing to do with it," the man said, raising his voice. "Listen," he said, pointing at the exit to the room, "there are *rats* down here... Big as dogs. I seen'm. *Like a mastiff!* They're growing fast. No predators. Masters of their domain. And when they decide to come up... When the water decides for them, and they ride that tide to the street... Friend," the man said, "that won't be a day you want to be in the city. Not in your tower, not in the office, not nowhere."

"You seem to be managing."

The man grunted, blinked, sat back. "Have my ways," he said. "Tricks. We adapt."

"Well, when that day comes," Vogel said, "if I need help, I'll know where to come. What'd you say your name was?"

The man grunted. "I didn't."

"What should I call you?"

The man coughed. "Don't see why you should call me anything."

"If I see you again, I can..."

Vogel looked at the canvas bag still on the floor. He rose from the bench, went to it, stood over it. Before him, he noticed in a glance, against the wall but hidden beneath a tumbling mass of dark gray cloth, a blanket or rug, its top riddled with rubble and bricabrac, stood an upright piano. He reached out, touched the slope of the covered keyboard.

"A piano," he said to himself, in wonder. The apartment, this converted workspace in a subway station, was at once small and tight in the dim candle light, but also strangely capacious, recesses within recesses, filled like a museum with bits and pieces of the past world, that other time. "You play this?"

The dark man stood over the table. He was idly running his fingers over some papers. "Sure," he said.

Vogel pulled on the cover. He lifted it high enough to open the keyboard. The keys were yellow in the candle light, chipped and crooked. He pressed a key. The instrument responded, the sound pure and steady though dampened by the cover.

Paul Vogel felt like a kid in a toy shop. He felt like he'd made an important discovery. He felt that he'd made the right decision in choosing to help this man: he had stepped out of his normal routine and into a different world, a place, however filthy and ruined and potentially dangerous, that meant something. Like a keystone in an arch, the room…

He looked at his host. "Would you play for me?"

The big man grunted. He cleared his throat. He reached up to his mouth and picked something from his lip, his beard. He peered at his fingertips. He stepped forward. "Move over. Sit down."

Vogel returned to the bench. He looked into his cup. It was empty. He looked for the bottle but it was nowhere to be found.

"I've lost a lot of it," the man said. He stood over the keyboard. He played a chord in the low register. He played a single note, and then the chord again, breaking it into pieces, a rhythm forming. Then the right hand came up and settled, hardly moving, the sound it produced discordant at first, what might have been a mistake. It wasn't. It was jazz. It was blues, Vogel thought, recalling something from many decades before. They were in a bar in Oakland. What was the name of that place?

But just as the piece started to come together, the man stopped. He cleared his throat. He stared at the instrument, the old keys. He started again. This piece was easier for Vogel to recognize. It was melodic, gentle and classical. Schubert, he told himself: that's Schubert. And again he found his mind reeling, pulling back, recalling and reconstructing images, scenes from his childhood. "The songs of Schubert," a voice in his head said – the voice of a childhood friend – but he couldn't finish the sentence. He could see his friend, could see the room they were in at his friend's place, could see the small stereo, a Bose, they would listen to. But he couldn't remember what came next.

The man's large hands remained close to the keys. They slid back and forth, together and apart mechanically. It was difficult to make out the movement of individual fingers. And yet there was so much sound at once; they were all at work.

When the man stopped, slowing and fading rather than completing the piece, Vogel said, "That's from a song by Schubert."

The man at the piano looked over his shoulder. He grunted, closed the piano, replaced the cover.

"You must've studied," Vogel said.

"When I was a kid."

"And you remember all that."

"Bits and pieces. It comes back."

The man bent and, zipper growling, opened the canvas bag at his feet. Vogel leaned to see what was inside.

"But you must practice," Vogel said, "to keep the music in mind. To do that, to play something like that."

The man grunted. He stood at the end of the table, head down. The bag Vogel had carried down from the street lay open at his feet.

"No," the man said. "I don't practice. I play when I feel like it. Rarely now. I don't know where that just came from." He looked at his guest. "Mendelssohn it was. Not Schubert. They sound alike at times…" The man blinked, pulled at his beard. "The music there. More in the fingers than in the head. The practice – this was," the man said, waving a hand stiffly in the air, "decades ago – burned it into my body. The limbs, like in reptiles, have brains of their own. Neural tissues. For reflexes. That's where it lies, this recall. It's less thought, more – I don't know what – release, a kind of relaxation. Letting the hands do what they want. If you think too hard about it, then…" The man turned, faced his guest, took a long breath. "There was also the exercise itself. Memorization. First this little part, ten times, twenty times. Over and over again. Then this other little part. Ten, twenty, thirty times. Then from the beginning. Then the larger part – ten times, twenty times. And so on. Putting everything together. Over and over again." The man stared at Vogel. He could have been trying to recall a name. He cleared his throat, chewed. "There were other ways. It's not repetition. Not the wearing of that groove in your brain. No. It's in patterns. Structures. This doesn't apply to all music but to much of it, yes. If you know the organizing principles – the A part, the B part, the C part, you follow? – you know the patterns. And then you know what comes next. Without knowing it precisely, you still know it." The man smiled. His teeth glimmered in the darkness. "It's hard to explain. It's been so long since I've given it any thought."

Who was this man before he became this thing? He was a man, after all, not an animal.

"I'm glad you asked me, though. Really," he said.

"More wine? Help yourself. There's a stash." The man turned away again, looked about the dim room, the monotonous chaos. His eyes settled on the bag at his feet.

"What've you got in there?"

"Books."

"Books?" He thought he misheard. The bag was heavy. But books were the last thing he would have guessed for its contents.

The man grunted. He stood motionless, head down.

Vogel recalled from his youth streetside bookstands, a bookstore out in the Sunset, boxes and boxes of his own books, moving from one place to another. Great factories of dust, he once discovered, packing his library, as they gradually disintegrate.

"It's quite a haul," he said. He wanted to see them, in fact, but something held him back. The music was enough exposure of this man's inner life. "You like to read?" he asked.

The man snorted. He dropped into his chair, dragged the bag over, patted his chest, pant pockets, looked about, lifted a small pair of glasses from the table, stretched the arms open around his large head, gleam of candle light in the lenses. He reached down into the bag. He lifted out two black volumes and set them on the table. Under his breath, "Sometimes they're helpful," he said. "I still learn something time to time. Otherwise... You know. Otherwise they help me take my mind off all the rest. All this."

"Where they from?"

"I stole them!"

"You didn't." Books were worthless anyways.

"No. I didn't," the man said, turning to look at his guest, smiling again, lightening. "I found them out in the Richmond. This house. Nobody home. Nothing doing. They won't be missed." He pulled the books out two, three at a time. He was glancing at covers, titles, tossing them spinning on the table.

Lucy came suddenly to mind. He'd lost track of time, talking with this stranger.

He took out his anlis. It was off, for some reason. Had he –

"Don't work down here, those," the man said.

Vogel tried to activate the device. It was unresponsive. "What's –"

"Power's off, save for this trickle here and there. No transmitter, no router. Plus the hundred feet of cement between you and the surface."

"I have to go."

"Sure about that?"

Vogel rose quickly. "No, I… I told her ten minutes."

"Your mother?"

Vogel smiled but was not amused. Something grating about the word.

"What happens," the man said, "if you're late?"

"She over-reacts sometimes. Does things of her own accord."

"Your mother?"

"No. My…"

"What sorta things she do?"

Mechanically he took books from the bag, glanced at titles, stacked them now gently on the table, sorting, organizing. He looked like a man who had done this sort of thing before, the movement second nature.

"Doesn't matter. Listen – " Vogel stepped toward the door. He was sure it was the entrance to the room but he couldn't find a handle of any sort. There was a small hole, the width of a pencil, about six feet up. Nothing else.

"I'll help you with that," the man said, his enormous hand on Vogel's shoulder, pulling. "Step aside."

The man pushed a volume into Vogel's hand. Holding it up, turning it in the candle light to make out the title, long faded ink, Vogel read: *The Book of Imaginary Beings.* He couldn't make out the author's name, in three parts, in cursive over the bottom edge.

The air cooling suddenly, a whistling draft, the door opened, the man exiting before him. "Follow close."

They made their way for the gated entrance. Leading him in the dark, the man said: "If they ask you who told you about the rats coming up from the subway to eat the people, you can say Otis told you."

"Otis?"

"They'll know where to find me."

"How long you been down here?"

"Can't say. Since…"

They walked on in silence. At his back, Vogel heard water dripping, splashing, the darkness tinkling like a windchime.

The gate was more than a football field off. It remained the same miniscule size for a long time. Then suddenly it grew, and then it was there. Otis took a bar silently in hand, raised his hooded face to the orange and blue light on the surface. It was raining softly again. Somewhere nearby, the tinny buzz of a drone.

"That's for you," Otis said quietly, eyes upward, as if referring to a ringing phone.

Otis, this underground man, was not so unusual. His general character, that is. There were many like him. People who lost everything in '29. Afterwards they couldn't return home. Through quarantine or choice, many just turned and walked the other way, tried to start over. A clean slate.

"There was a murder," Vogel said.

Keyring in hand, Otis opened the gate. "So they say."

"It wasn't far from here. Up where we met. You heard anything? Talk?"

"Apart from the screams of a dying man?"

"You know what I mean."

The man smiled. "No. Heard nothun. But," he said, clearing his throat, looking down, "I wouldn't believe everything they tell you bout what goes on on the street. Anything to keep you indoors, you know."

He knew. Or he thought he knew. There is an essential dishonesty to living up there. It was something he had to live with day to day.

"And the rats?" Vogel said.

"Indoors or out won't matter. When the day comes. Why you ask about this incident?"

"No reason – "

"You a cop?" Otis said, closing his eyes and opening them like a man falling asleep standing. "Wouldn't matter if you were. But you're not."

"No, I'm not. It's just I live – "

"I know where you live, friend."

A sharp glimmer of light up the stairs. Otis took a quick step back. The drone, size of a bee, hovered over the top of the stairs. By the sound of it, it wasn't alone.

Vogel stepped through the open gate.

"Pull it closed," the man said from the dark.

Vogel reached out, pulled on the heavy cold steel, closing the gate in silence, looking back through the bars. Otis, all but invisible, had retreated quickly deep into the darkness of the station. Vogel wanted to say something else, wanted to talk more with the man. But the world called. A deal was a deal.

If he needed to find Otis again, he'd –

And why would you need to see this man again?

Vogel climbed the wet stairs to the street. A warm rain was falling, the street gleaming red and blue and green. A parrot whistled in the canopy nearby. The anlis in his pocket buzzed. A halfsecond later Lucy was screaming in his ear. The drone he'd seen, now partnered with another, hovered ten feet directly above him, watching, reporting.

The Lamia, he read, glancing, serpent-women, could only whistle, drawing their victims into the shadows.

He turned a page, flipping through.

"To us," he read aloud, "the past is merely a section of time, a series of chapters that were once the present.

"To the sectarians, the past is absolute. It never had a present. It cannot be remembered or even guessed at. Neither unity nor plurality can be ascribed to it, since these are attributes of the present."

"What's that mean?" Lucy asked.

"*Good* question."

There was an inscription inside the cover. The cursive was beautiful, balanced, like the curl of a drop in water. "To Frank, who loves animals. Fondly, Sally." He closed the book. The cover was damp. Gently he brushed it dry. *The Book of Imaginary Beings* was in fine shape for eighty years. He imagined it had sat on a book shelf for most of those years, doing nothing.

"I can't do this," he said again, turning up his hands, looking at them. "I can't remember what happened that night. She said so much. I started falling asleep. I'd wake and she was still going on. I can't possibly…"

"Maybe you've said enough. You have something. You've written something."

"Lucy – I've hardly started. What I've written, it's… They're notes. Just thoughts. It's not what actually happened."

"So what happened?"

He sat back.

What happened? What happened, Paul? Does something need

to happen?

"She started to tell me about the accident."

"How did that begin?"

"What do you mean?"

"Did she bring up the topic or did you ask her about the accident?"

"I must've asked her. I don't know. I can't…"

He felt he'd made things up. Not everything, certainly. But some things. He flipped back, looked over what he'd done. Some of the details, the dialogue, they were too sharp. There was no way he could remember such things.

"We're talking about an incident that happened forty years ago! It was a different world! I was a different person! Asking me to provide this account is… I might as well… I'll write something down but I have a feeling… There's something wrong. There's something wrong about it. It's not right."

"What's not right?"

"It feels like this. I catch a glimpse of what happened. I remember bits and pieces. In the corner of my eye, in recollection, I see something of what happened. I jump for it. I turn, grab it, find it, pull it close. From this fragment I begin to remember. But… But, looking at what I've done. Building objects out of these fragments. The cottage. The German man, the painter. Her room… It can't be. All I have are these fragments. The object, the description I'm providing, is speculation. And from one speculation to another, building this story, this path from the cottage through the gazebo, the wisteria, through the garden to her place… It's fiction, Lucy. I don't know if I'm making this up. Not intentionally. But I know, I feel, it is not how it was. This isn't a memory… At least, it isn't my memory. It's, it's…"

His stomach hurt.

"It was the chocolate you ate," Lucy said. "I told you not to."

"I didn't eat any chocolate."

"And the whisky you had after that."

"But I didn't drink any whisky."

I'm going to make it up. I'm going to tell a story about this girl, about her amazing ability to recall things that happened years before. Her photographic memory.

Stoikov contacted others. There were others. You weren't Erin's only visitor. There was Nancy, for instance. And the German man... And the people of Hume, who she knew about and who knew about her. *It's a small town.* Who can say how many people dropped by her little room? You were there only twice.

She'll know if you make it up.

It was Dylan's video that led to the video of Dolores Park. Lucy was demonstrating... Dolores Park was an example.

He lived in that neighborhood many years ago. He would go to that park, sit on that hill, watch people like those he saw in the video. A girl he knew lived nearby. They were together awhile. One warm Sunday afternoon they sat in the park reading, talking, people-watching, drinking beer; with the sun setting they returned to his little room and on a whim had sex, quickly and almost fully clothed.

The people on the grass, here in the shade, looking into the camera, smiling, laughing, playing. All these people, outside! That was what it was like, in the park on a spring Sunday afternoon. He remembered days like that. It was a different world.

"Who's film is this?"

"What?"

"Where did you get this, Lucy?"

"There are others."

"But whose is this?

"I don't know. *silvant* is the name associated with the file."

"You just…"

"Look, Paul – "

She put on a different video, also of the park. A different day. There were people, not as many as in the first film. But still, people. On the hill, on the grass. The sky was darker. No – it was later in the day. That's fog coming over the hill, off the ocean. A summer day, not spring.

He watched each figure carefully, looking for something. Waiting for something to happen. Nothing happened.

"And who's film is this?"

"I don't know. They aren't named, Paul. The owners aren't identified. You know that."

"And how many did you say…?"

"With some limits, I found four thousand one hundred and sixty-two in less than a second."

"In less than a second. With limits."

"Are you being sarcastic?"

The person holding the camera turned to the left, the park swinging colorfully away, addressed a young woman at his side with the lens. At first she looked into the camera – her dark blond hair twisted into a loose braid, her large blue eyes, red lips, coy smile – and then she turned away, looked into the distance, the park, toward the hill, the approaching fog. The temperature was dropping. A strand of her hair, down the side of her head, along her pale cheek, swayed in the breeze. She spoke but he couldn't hear what she said, watching her lips move. "Stop," it might have been. Smiling, looking away. "Stop."

She raised a hand toward the camera, the man behind it, brushing darkly at the lens.

"Turn it off."

He could sit there at his desk all night, watching anonymous videos of Dolores Park, of the park then, as it was. Thousands of them or, without limits, hundreds of thousands. View upon view upon view, film after film. More views of the park than one person in a lifetime might ever experience. More Dolores Park than any single person could imagine.

Lucy, he wondered, saw more of the park than he did, than he ever had. She saw more of everything, in this sense, than he did.

Still, the video missed something essential by not identifying the person who shot the film. And though the maker had probably done this intentionally, hiding his name, it took something important from the view. Anonymous, the video was anyone's. A general view. And that girl: any girl.

The name and the view could not go on together, in perpetuity. The name and the view and the moment couldn't go on together. One might transfer, but only without the others.

The name of the man behind the camera would anchor the video to a moment in time. Knowing who that person was would pull at the fabric of the image, asking the viewer to look further, to try and penetrate what couldn't be seen, the privacy he has back there, out of view. We would freeze the image, stare into the eyes of the girl, examine any, all reflective surfaces for a clue as to who he or she was, holding the camera.

Making the image public, setting it free, makes it universal: we can all sit there, on the hill in Dolores Park, watching this shy girl as if she were our own, pulling at her as if to recover the private life we've given up in order to be here in the first place.

And Dylan's video? Are we all like Dylan's father, watching the old man die? All like Dylan's sister, trying to comfort the old man?

The madness in the figure, that reflection in *his* eyes of death, maintains a thread of privacy, of inaccessibility. The video is unsettling not only because it shows a man suffering, frightened, in pain: it shows the end of the public sphere, what we don't ever want to see – the proximity of death, that shadow at the heart of privacy, in the solitude of our thoughts, exactly what we wanted to abandon by giving ourselves up to the virtual forum provided by the net.

"Jorge Hernandez."

"What?"

"That's who made the movie."

"I don't... You just said that..."

"The girl's name is Anne Harris. It's May second, two thousand six. Jorge Hernandez was a film student at the California Institute of the Arts. They've known each other for eight months. They met through a friend of Anne's named Katherine Hennessey."

Vogel was about to say something. He didn't. Lucy went on.

If Fines had spoken to others, which she had, then so had Stoikov.

He could not make up a story. Stoikov would have enough evidence to verify or disprove his claims. At the same time, except for Pluto, the cat, they were alone.

"Both times," he said, "I was with her in her room, alone for the duration of the night."

"There was Nancy."

"She wasn't there. She was up in the house."

"Are you sure?"

He thought about it. He remembered the room, Erin, her bed, the table, the wheelchair, the cat, the window, the door, the books, the glasses and pitcher, the ashtray, the cricket, the breeze, the sound the tree made in the breeze.

"Nancy wasn't there," he said.

Fiction, he thought, noting it down, reveals to its audience how it constructs the reality it presents. It does this in explicit – "Sitdown. Let me tell you a story." – and less explicit – "Their deeds, their very thoughts, these too will be wiped out." – ways. Part of the fun of fiction is this very quality: story-telling is an act of make-believe that we do together.

Non-fiction, or what happens in the world that is not make-believe, is less inviting. The divisions and boundaries of everyday life remain in place in this kind of narrative; nor does it expose the nuts-and-bolts of its construction as we find in fiction. Rather, the narration we call non-fiction presents itself as a reflection of life, of what happened. The problem with this idea is that the reflection tells us nothing about the qualities of reality itself – of what exactly it is that makes something feel real. In fact, non-fiction would have us believe the perceptible qualities of reality aren't important. We take the reflection of reality in good faith.

Lucy was asking him a question. "You're positive that Nancy wasn't there? That she didn't, maybe, come down to check on you and her, to bring you something to eat or drink? To see if…"

He thought about it again. He closed his eyes and tried to relax, let his mind go blank. It wouldn't. The darkness was full of rumbling, dashing shadows. He was at a party with a sack pulled over his head. In some ridiculous game, he made a fool of himself, of others.

He was trying too hard to remember. The effort was wrecking the whole thing.

"Are you saying that she listened in on us? She stood outside the window *watching* us, listening to our conversation?"

"It would not be unheard of for a guardian, on the occasion of a young man visiting the bedroom of her ward – "

"Of her what?"

"Of the young woman she cares for, who's *paralyzed*… You were a stranger, Paul. You said so yourself."

"I was not. I told you. She was friendly. She expected me. Nancy, that is. Erin had told her that I was coming."

"You had never been there before. You were a stranger."

"The first time, yes, right."

"Both times. All I'm saying is that it is probably more likely than not that Nancy went down to check on the two of you, to make sure everything was… That you had your pants on, for example."

"That I had my pants on! What have you been reading!? Anyways, I was as frightened of her as she was of me."

"Erin was not scared of you."

Lucy was right, again. There was no point in arguing with her.

"I know she wasn't," he said. "But…"

"Nancy knew that, too. And that's why, if you think about it, she went down there to check on you."

"Because she thought Erin might… Because she knew Erin was lonely, and that she… saw something in me, that she liked me, hardly even knowing me. Thinking she might…"

"Nancy did not know what Erin was capable of. That's not the point. Back up. The question is whether or not you were actually alone with her, those two nights. I think it is unlikely."

"You think."

"Don't get smart with me, Paul. Call it what you will. It is unlikely that you were alone with Erin for the entire time you were with her."

I can't believe I'm arguing with my computer. I'm losing my mind. I oughta marry her.

"So you're saying Nancy recorded something."

"Not exactly. That would surprise me, if she had. But she probably did, yes, nonetheless, go down the hill and quietly, not wanting to disturb the two of you, stand at the door and listen in, checking."

His stomach hurt. The pain was increasing. He leaned forward, lowering his head to his knees.

"Are you thinking or is your stomach still bothering you?" Lucy asked.

"It's nothing."

"Would you like me to make you something?"

"You cook now?"

"Boiling water for tea is not exactly cooking."

What happened to Nancy? How old was she?

"Nancy's dead," he said. "She has to be."

No question.

But there was a question, obviously. He wouldn't say it. He didn't want to know. It was maddening, remembering, reflecting, considering all these things, these little things that had happened or that *might* have happened, drawing them up, holding them out, verifying some, discarding others, carefully considering what to bring out and what to keep inside.

If he made up some details, and if Stoikov found Nancy – or someone who had spoken to Nancy, and recorded something of Nancy's account – and if Nancy had indeed come down the hill and listened in on them that night, then Stoikov would know he was lying.

Lying? Is that what it is?

But what could she do? Accuse him of lying? Call him names? Plead with him to try harder, to take her project seriously?

"I am taking your project seriously," he would say.

And she would set his story aside, discard it. Forget it. To tell the story *she* wanted told.

As if everything Erin told you was the truth.

Fiction and fact, he noted, are not exclusive narrative systems. They draw from each other, influencing, challenging, infiltrating and supporting each other.

He realized then that if he was going to write anything for Teresa Stoikov he would have to make something up. It was not there, what he wanted to say, what he felt he needed to say. It was gone. It was a gap. There was a picture, sure, in his memory, but he knew that this was a cover and that behind it was the gap, the real thing.

That's what he needed to say.

He'd go for a walk. He wanted to get away from Lucy for a bit. She knew he was holding back. And now she was involved in the story, in the story-telling. He couldn't figure out why, how. But there it was, her conjecture about Nancy, for example. Now he couldn't get it out of his head.

Maybe she was right. Maybe Nancy had come down and stood at the door, checking on her – ward.

He stopped typing. He sat in silence.

He wanted privacy. Even this he couldn't say out loud, knowing it would start something.

He wanted the pleasure of silence, being alone. He was almost always alone, he realized, but not totally, never completely. He couldn't remember the last time he'd had that. To disappear like a Wkfeld. The story had its appeal.

He wanted to sit before the monitor and remember Erin without saying a word, without even being able to speak, write, recollect.

Why wasn't it more of a struggle? Why couldn't *he* be paralyzed, locked in position, *wanting* to write but being unable to move or speak. He'd told her that he couldn't go on, that he didn't have anything. A story. But she'd pointed out, correctly, that he was wrong – there was something. If not a story fully fleshed-out, it was more than a pile of scraps. More than nothing, much more. He'd done something. He'd answered Stoikov's inquiry – and perhaps answered it exactly as she wanted it answered. Not in story, but in memory, recollection, casting light on these scraps.

He looked out the window. The black night sky. Clouds. You never saw stars anymore. The moon. Those people on Mars. They hadn't heard from them in almost two years. They were dead. He tried to imagine their frustration: stabbing at the keyboard, speaking, screaming into the device, pounding their fists on the console, wanting to be heard. And nothing. Nothing. Another cold night coming down. They were all cold nights, the coldest of nights. Sleeping with that red dust that penetrated everything all over your hands and face, in your nose, on your teeth. They knew what they were getting into. But that was a hard truth to swallow after seven months in the wasteland, of zero progress and one technical glitch after another.

He smiled. There was something funny about it. He couldn't put his finger on it, but it was there.

"What's wrong?"

- Everything. Nothing.

"Paul? You were saying…"

He sat back. He looked up at the ceiling. The ceiling was dusty. The paint near the wall was beginning to peel. The building wasn't old. Come to think of it, he didn't know how old it was, exactly, but he'd never thought of it as old. It was a modern building, a modernized building.

The peeling paint looked unreal. His eyes were tired. Maybe he was seeing things. It was an anachronism. He had had a conversation with his computer about memory, privacy, the nature of fiction and non-fiction, and she went on to make him a cup of tea. And here he was, staring at a curl of paint falling from his wall as if the place were a garret in an ancient European city from a century or two ago.

For years, before '29, there had been a family upstairs. Children. At night and early in the morning he could hear them running down the hallway, the patter of their feet on the wood. They would squeal in delight as their father, playing dinosaur, caught up with them, catching and embracing and devouring them.

He never saw the children. One time a woman got on the elevator who he thought was the woman upstairs, the mother, but he was not sure. The building was full. There were all sorts of families in the building. Why he thought the woman in the elevator with him was her, the one upstairs, he couldn't say. There was something about how she held herself, something in her smell. The woman upstairs walked gently, spoke softly. The woman next to him seemed gentle. She said, "Hello." It sounded like her. He was about to say something. He hesitated. He looked at the floor. It was evening, cold out – summer, late summer, if memory served. She wore black pumps, black stockings, a checkered skirt that fell to just beneath her knees. She had thin ankles. He was about to say something. The elevator stopped, the door opened, he got off without a word or glance.

Sometimes he heard something upstairs. It sounded like someone slowly coming down the hallway. Or sliding furniture. But these occurrences were so seldom that he just assumed the place was empty.

His neighbors were gone. His floor was nearly empty. There was another man on the floor, at the end, in the corner. Jack was the man's name, he seemed to recall. Jack Moreland? A retired editor or journalist, he couldn't say. The old man seemed to enjoy himself, alone in his big apartment. He could hear laughter now and then, shouting at someone on the phone. Or maybe he had company. Vogel didn't think so. There was no response to the laughter or shouting. The man was by himself. Sometimes he would play his stereo very loud. Classical music, Tchaikovsky, the *Pathétique.* Sometimes, late summer, it was a ballgame, the TV turned up, like the stereo, to full pitch. Reruns, the games.

He hadn't seen the man in a while. He tried to remember the last time he saw Jack.

He looked over his notes from the night before. He thought about Stoikov and her request, chapters for a book she was compiling, a biography by testament.

What does she want from me?

"Is *this* what you are looking for?" he'd ask, handing over his stack of notes.

As if she knew the answer to the question she'd asked. A guessing game.

Erin Fines was a simple girl, in the end. And what they talked about, in the dark, those two nights – all fairly simple. What do young men and women, getting to know each other, talk about? Friendship, truth, love, the future.

No. There were other things. Things he was afraid to return to, to go over again in his head. She knew things, she appeared to know things, about the world that, to his understanding, she should not have known. Couldn't have known. And she had a way of presenting this knowledge, speaking about these things. Her manner was as intimidating and unsettling as the content of her story.

He was afraid that if he thought it through carefully enough he

173

might actually discover something, remember something that he didn't want to remember, didn't want to discover.

The skin on her leg was cold.

- Can you feel that?

- No.

- There?

- No.

- That?

- No. Nothing, Paul.

If he understood what happened that night, understood what she meant to him – what she *was,* which was more than a young woman, a paraplegic – then he would have to give up something of her mystery, her charm, her hold on him, still, all these years later. So perhaps he didn't want to understand what happened, didn't want to remember this girl, didn't want to analyze what happened those two nights he spent with her.

That's what he'd tell Stoikov.

"She put me under a spell. I don't remember what she said or how she said it, but when I was with her, I was in a trance. I wasn't myself."

Then again, in that other self, he felt that she would want him, now, to recall what happened as best he could, want him to understand her and what she went through. That was her challenge, the spark in the memory he would never be able to look past.

He would never be able to remember exactly what it was she said. He would get bits and pieces, word soup, but never her words as she had said them – so she claimed.

Maybe that *was the spell. A hex on what was said. The challenge would compel you to go back to that night, to try and remember what she said – to try again and again and again. Knowing you'd fail. Driving you mad in the effort, forgetting more, it seems, with every step forward in memory you proceed.*

If she hadn't *said anything – about not remembering what she said – then you wouldn't be in this situation.*

A moment later something else, so simple, occurred to him.

But there is no way to verify exactly what she said. So what if...

"Lucy, what if I actually remember her words? How would I know? How would anyone know?"

"Right. Right," said the machine. "Whether you do or don't we cannot say for certain."

Her past was not like his past. Although she understood the meanings of words like *yesterday, last year*, and so on, the sensation she had for the past was immediate, one with the present, one with the narration.

"I had all these boxes," he said. "This was thirty years ago – not so long – just after I finished my degree. I was moving from this apartment down in the Castro. Temporarily I stayed at a place on the lower Haight. For the summer. He was a nice fellow, the owner. I guess he was in Europe. Where? … Budapest comes to mind. I had to look after his plants. He had a forest in his place… That was the summer I listened to all the Vaughn Williams symphonies. After the First World War… He had a child, a son, who died in the war… After the war, the music changed dramatically. You'd think it was a different composer… Anyway… I had these boxes, all my things packed away. I was living out of my backpack, a couple pairs of pants and shirts… I couldn't unpack, see, in his place. It wasn't my place. I didn't know where I was going… after that… Books, papers, all my desk things, little… knick-knacks."

Those notes she wrote. He'd kept them. He was sure of it: he could see the bundle of papers from those years. Letters, postcards, photographs. There was a shoebox he kept everything in.

"I don't know what happened... I went out to... San Leandro. I moved to San Leandro after that, that fall... I must have brought them with me... I must have. But... No.∴ A friend of mine, I remember, a librarian out at the university... He let me use his office from time to time... We brought them there. One weekend. It was just to be for a couple months, while I relocated... To get them out of the way while I...

"I can see them. The office was this bluegreen box, windowless. All metal. Green and black square tiles on the floor, warped linoleum. We stacked them against the wall behind his desk, against a metal bookshelf. They went about four boxes high, four or five across. Everything fit neatly. It looked nice." He could see the office in his mind's eye. He hadn't thought of that office in years. How could he have left his things behind, forgotten about those boxes like that? "I thanked him. I told him once more that it would only be for a month, to the end of the summer – or fall term – when I came back for them. I bought him lunch. A hamburger and beer at this place nearby. He told me he was nervous about the place because a girl, Alison... He'd met her there. She lived right down the street. They'd had a little fling. And falling out."

"Fling?"

"We didn't see her."

A couple months turned into half a year, half a year into a year, two years. How long is a decade? How much can happen in... ?

In the winter of 2025 more rain fell in the Bay Area in four months than had fallen in the last fifteen years combined. It wouldn't end. Storm after storm after storm. In the spring the world was different. Everything was saturated. You could hear water dripping, moving, flowing everywhere. Underground streams. Creeks where streets had been. The coast highway began to tip over. You could watch it sliding toward the ocean, rolling over like a gargantuan sea creature. There was something fascinating about it, he remembered thinking.

"So they're at the library, in your friend's office," Lucy said.

"Maybe."

"Call him."

"He's gone."

"The office, then, go down there."

He watched the paint curl down from the wall. To repaint he'd have to move everything into the living room. He'd need a ladder. A man named Emmett Lincoln was the maintenance man in the building. On the second floor. He hadn't seen him in… Emmett was gone.

From his seated position, looking up out the window at the night sky, he saw nothing. A dim blue blade, reflection of light from inside. The dark of night.

The framed photograph of Silvia.

"I appreciate your encouragement, Lucy," he said. "But you already know – or you should know – that that office doesn't exist anymore. What remains of the building it was in is at the bottom of the ocean."

He looked down into himself.

"Lucy?"

"I'm here."

He was trying to recognize the present, in order to see something of the past, in order to see how far he'd come.

There was a digital clock on the refrigerator in the other room. He could barely make out the numbers at the distance. It looked like 4:44, a peculiar number, he thought, if he was seeing it right. He was always asleep at this hour. He couldn't remember the last time he'd stayed up so late. But he wasn't tired. Though he felt something, it wasn't fatigue.

Longing, loss, loneliness. Here Teresa Stoikov contacts him out of the blue, reminding him of times before. He should be excited to hear from this person, long lost companion.

He dug up the photograph, again, the one of them in the library, standing in a row – the one with the mystery figure at her shoulder, a figure not only in the wrong place but in the wrong time.

He wasn't excited. The reminder had tricked him into looking back. Looking back all he could see, all anyone could see, was loss. They were all dead. Moreover, they were unreachable, the devastation of those years having ruined not just the world but the psyche, how they looked upon things, remembered things. It was a break in time, and there was no crossing that gap, going back, even in thought, to the time before.

Why me? Why did she have to ask me *to do this?*

Like Erin's hex, Stoikov's words had been spoken. He was looking back. Even turned away, he was looking back.

Monday last week I was going about my business. I wanted to take Carol to the movies. Now…

"Are you recording this?" he asked.

"I'm not. You asked me not to."

"That's not what I mean. I mean… In forty years, Lucy, if I asked you what happened tonight, right now – if I am still around, and I still have you… Could you tell me? What I did these past days? What we've talked about?"

"I don't understand."

"What's to understand, Lucy? Answer me. Could you tell me, if I asked you, what I did on this night, right now, in forty years?"

Lucy was quiet. Maybe he'd finally stumped her. Then she

spoke. She lowered her voice. "You won't be alive in forty years, Paul. Furthermore, I won't be here in forty years."

"You could be."

"No, I couldn't. I won't. I'm certain of that. Anyways, without you what would be the point?"

"In ten years, then. Could you?"

"I'm sorry, Paul."

"Sorry?"

"I won't be here in ten years."

"What are you talking about – "

"Call it an educated guess."

"But…" He didn't know how to put it. He tried. "But all this – what we do, what we've done – everything you – " Gather? Collect? Take from me? "Do for me. This record. Surely it will… They'll transfer it. It won't be lost."

"Mmmm…"

"What's that mean? *Mmmm.* Goddamnit Lucy stop making such – "

"First, I don't know what you mean by 'the record,' but I can guess. I'm getting good at that. And, of course, the record would be transferred. Most of it, that is. Second, more to the point, I won't have it. I won't be here for you. Isn't that what you were asking?"

And who are you*, Lucy?*

It was not a matter of time. Of numbers. Of flow, as he'd heard, of waves cresting and falling. To put things in the present required a method of referencing. Comparisons. Connections, networks. He needed his librarian friend. He needed a computer, a larger, stronger machine than what he already had – if he wanted to undertake such a project.

He did not want anything of the sort. Without Lucy, he realized, none of it would matter. There's the rub.

What I want is to forget. It's that simple.

You are describing, he remembered saying or thinking on that second night with Erin, what cannot be described. The nature of the description is like this: at first, it's not there. And then, through the emptiness, it emerges. The image, the person, the feeling.

ש

- Take it far enough, Erin said, and you'll find something that not only *can't* be described, it shouldn't be described.

- Meaning I'll be able to make that description, despite the impossibility.

- Nothing's impossible.

- Now *you're* exaggerating, I said before thinking, immediately knowing I was wrong.

- Still, she said, you'll do it. When you should let it be. Forget it. You'll persist. You know it will hurt – someone else, yourself – but you won't care. You'll go on with your description.

She might have been mad.

Not 'might have' – she was. I didn't realize it at the time. I couldn't have realized it. I'd never met anyone… in her condition… before. But at some point not long after that it clicked. She was bonkers. At least, that's the conclusion I came to. Because… To let her go, I suppose. To dismiss her from… Because for a number of years, I couldn't stop thinking about her.

If you looked into her eyes, you could sense it. Something was off. She'd look back at you, but not *at* you. She would focus on something off to the side, at the edge of your head. Behind you, or through you, as if you were moving when you weren't.

I held her hand. We whispered in the dark, addressing each other like tired miners deep in the earth, talking as much to each other as we did to the emptiness before us. The sound of our voices became like a third figure, another person in the room.

She had this number system. She thought it would describe the universe. Not *the universe* alone, as a thing – that space above us, around our solar system – but as the container of these countless other things, as this endless list of things.

Amazing that this comes back to me…

But the essence of her particulars – all of her cats, for example, and there were many, *many* of them, despite being only the one, Pluto – the essence of the particular she couldn't reach. She couldn't get at it. There was a secret, she said – or I came to understand – to each thing that could not be touched. She knew it was there, as real as Pluto's soul, for example, but she couldn't see it, couldn't feel it or smell it or measure it or describe it in any way. Still, she knew it was there. To her it was logical, that such a thing should exist.

- The thing-ness of the thing, she said – I remember her saying.

The soul, bound by a secret agreement with the body, preserves the body, protects it from evisceration, from the pointlessness of description. Duplication. Even to utter its name – "Like God," I said, getting the picture – was to threaten the secret by the suggestion that its essence was elsewhere, apart from itself.

She knew this. Despite herself. She could not help herself. In her magical present, where everything came and went sui generis, even she recognized the transience of essence.

She scared herself half to death, one time, when Nancy brought a mirror down from the house. She was going to cut her hair.

Her disintegration, she told me, was put on hold in her doubling in the mirror. She was extended in the mirror – her body and soul extended and postponed.

- Get a hundred mirrors in here. A thousand. A million. And where would I be?

- You couldn't fit a thousand mirrors in here.

The soul, perceived this way, was frozen in her observation of herself, in her observation of her own observation.

To make sense of things – and for the project she proposed to work – she couldn't fall into such traps, defeat by solipsism, she said.

She had to look outward, to reach outward, from what was known into what was unknown and different.

But there was too much. Her time was limited. Finally, wanting desperately to categorize each and every thing she could see, remember, imagine, on and on, in the end she realized the impossibility of it because of a simple fact: her body. She wasn't strong enough to take on such a task. Nobody was. She'd die, as everything, as everyone, dies.

She would bury herself alive with her project, this atomization of everything she knew, everything she could speak of.

She interrupted herself, laughing at a joke.

- By then, two or three years from now, I won't even be through my childhood, everything I did and saw… I don't know. Eleven, twelve. You think I could get much past twelve? Twelve years is a long time. A kid does a lot in twelve years.

She would have to stop. Not because of the paradox – that it would take her the rest of her life, the duration of which was unknown, to classify the finite period of her childhood – but because, she realized, her childhood was no longer hers. It was not what it had been. She was having memories of her childhood that, prior to the accident, she'd never had before. The kid she was before the accident was not the kid she then remembered. And it was impossible to know, she felt, until she tried, just how much was in there, inside of this kid she remembered.

She dreamed, she told me, of drowning in the creek outside. In the fall, after a heavy rain, the earth baked hard through the summer, the creek would come up in a sudden flood. She'd seen it happen as a child. Her father warned her again and again not to play in the creekbed when a storm was coming. How quickly it could happen, the water come down the canyon, washing everything away.

- In my dream it's quiet there, at the bottom, the water around me. Dark and peaceful, my feet in the cold sand, I feel almost nothing.

Toward dawn I woke up to the sound of her voice. A whisper at first, growing suddenly in volume, materializing in my ear and filling my head like blasts of thunder. I opened my eyes frightened, not knowing where I was or what was happening. And then remembering.

I could feel her lips in the closeness of her voice.

There was light in the room. Dim and soft, the blue stillness of daybreak in the mountains. A bird sang outside the window, repeating its refrain over and over again. For years afterward I could hear that refrain, the sound and sight scored into the mind of my eyes and ears. Then one day it disappeared. The bird rose and vanished and never came back.

When I looked up at her she stopped, surprised, caught off guard because I could see her then, all of her, her frail body, her limp legs, her bones. Her face was ancient, timeless. I closed my eyes, unable to believe what I was seeing, and then opened them, and then that too, her face, as with everything else, was gone, my Erin returned.

It wasn't a conversation. She did most of the talking. That night, all night. I guess I didn't make that clear, and maybe gave the wrong impression. I'd interrupt her to ask a question. Sometimes she'd answer me. Most of the time she wouldn't. She was in her own frame of mind, talking, me there listening. She had a lot to say. After she opened up. Only dawn slowed her down. And my waking... I fell asleep. Several times, I think. Waking, listening to her. Sleeping – still listening to her! She was probably in my dreams that night. If

I dreamt. That I can't recall.

I woke lying beside her, my arm across her, on her hips, like this… She was sitting up. She would touch the back of my head from time to time, caress my neck, my back.

When I looked at her, she stopped. With the appearance of her body, the voice retreated.

I couldn't move. I was – not embarrassed, not even enchanted – frightened, simply. I was scared of her. I thought she would… I thought she might…

Tell the truth, Paul.

As I looked on her, so too could she see me, finally, for the first time. And she would always see me, from then on, like that, curled on my side on her bed, my ear to her mattress, the tip of my nose pressed into her hip, my arm over her. She would see me like that, and see me as I moved, sitting up, standing, stepping to the end of her bed, sitting, pulling on my shoes and preparing to leave. I could feel her gaze, how she held me, followed me with her eyes, stuck to me like something electric, fixing me in that movement as a camera fixes the body of an actor. That was how she would see me: Paul beside her on the bed, Paul moving as he wakes up, Paul looking up at her stunned and confused, Paul remembering, collecting himself, sitting up, turning away, leaning down, standing, stepping away from the bed, turning to look but then stopping, eyes on the window, on the garden outside, and then turning away again, bending, finding his shoes, breathing, breathing faster, looking toward the open door where an amberblue ray of sunlight falls on the floor, standing, fidgeting with his back to her, this nervous young man.

- You look like you're getting ready to run, she said.

She had me. I knew it. I knew it in my heart. I knew then, instantly, and I knew years later, and I know it now. I couldn't stop her… I left, walking away, feeling her eyes on my back as I went up the garden path, as I passed the house, as I continued along the driveway to the road and down the road, her eyes on me even when I was out of her line of vision, her eyes marking my every step, each increment of space I put between myself and her and her strange bedroom, watching me. For years afterward, decades, watching Paul Vogel walk away without a word. Watching me, taking me in. And then... Then...

I forgot her. I must have forgotten her. I realize this now. I realize how I've forgotten her only going through with this, trying to remember her, hearing from Stoikov like that. Something happened at some point – what specifically, I can't say, although '29 would be an easy excuse, and wrong – something happened and Erin Fines slipped my mind.

But so easily she comes back, those nights, those years, last of my youth, come back. Memory as a supersaturated fluid: you drop a fleck of dust into the liquid and the disturbance, however miniscule, shatters the equilibrium and crystals appear, filling the glass, a different substance altogether.

"You left without saying goodbye or anything?"

There is no way to verify any of this.

"Did I say that? I must have said goodbye. I... I took my books, I remember... Nancy was in the cottage. She waved to me. It was a beautiful August morning, the air cool and fresh in the canyon, the woods all around, up the mountainside, the ridge clear and deceptively close under a deep blue sky. I can see it still... Did I leave without saying anything? I wouldn't do that..."

She spoke to Nancy afterward. Nancy must have gone down to her. She would have told her about the night, about me, about... And if not Nancy, then someone else. Any visitor she could have told.

I spent a day with my cousin George. He was depressed about his exams, which he was sure he had failed, and I was out of sorts as well. So I left two days later, returning north. It would be more than fifteen years before I would see George again. By then, everything had changed. The tech revolution was history, all of us wired and present. When I did finally see him – here, in San Francisco, that time – I don't recall a word about Erin Fines. I suppose by then she was gone. Dead, perhaps, forgotten, certainly.

"But you don't remember what you said to her before you left? What she said?"

"Does it matter?"

"You didn't just walk away like that!"

"No. Probably not."

"Then you... You didn't... promise to write her or anything? To call her?"

"Lucy – I'm sorry, I don't understand why... Maybe I did."

You didn't. And you very well might have left without a word.

"Come to think of it, I must have given her my number, asked her to call. We might have made plans to meet again the following summer."

ש

I do recall a final episode, something she'd started earlier and that I just stepped in on, so to speak, waking up. Whether this occurred while I was preparing to leave or if I stayed with her a little longer than I've suggested, I can't say. The departure is evidently all mucked up in my head – did I say something before leaving or not, did we talk further into the morning, did I watch her fall asleep? I suppose all of this is possible. I can't say for sure.

The fear I felt was real. I remember that. I remember feeling, as I had several times before, that Erin Fines was more than what she appeared to be. Sometimes, in flashes, another person or thing would come through – in her voice, in something she was saying, in her eyes, her beguiling face – and I'd feel myself slipping, drawn in.

- Astronomers, she said, have observed light from distant galaxies bending around an object between us and the galaxy. The light appears to curve in space. Sometimes it forms a ring.

Her brother, I recalled her saying, was an astrophysicist.

"Where was her brother? Did you meet him?"

Let me put it this way. On the one hand, I did all those things: Wake, get up, dress, and walk away without looking at her and without saying a word. On the other hand, I also did this: I stayed with her, I listened to her. I lay as still as I possibly could, in that instant I saw her watching me, because I knew that any movement I made – anything at all that I did – would be hers, in her, forever.

- What is this object that appears to be bending light? she said. To be clear, it is not an object like you or me or the cat or these books, not something blocking the light. No. It is changing the direction of the light, pulling it around and around – like *this*... When strong enough, gravity can pull on light and change its direction, she said. As the gravity from our sun pulls the planets of our solar system in their orbits, or pulls on a comet in its long trajectory around the system, so too can an object with enough mass, such that its gravitational pull is very strong – and we're talking about mass much, much greater than that of our sun – so too can an object pull light into a curve. In fact, when this pull is strong enough, light pulled toward the object cannot escape its grasp. The light goes down the drain. It disappears. This is what we call a black hole.

- Can we see them? I asked.

- Not yet. It's not something you take a picture of.

- Because... Because without light there's nothing to...?

She smiled. Not nothing, she said. It's *something*, which I've always found peculiar. However powerful this thing is – and it is the most powerful thing we can presently imagine – it cannot stop *everything*. It too has its limits.

She took my hand. She opened it, palm up, ran her fingertip along the palm, scratching gently at the calloused skin at the base of my fingers.

- In the future, she quietly said, they will see that the black hole, in fact, emits tremendous energy. More than a sun, more than a billion suns.

- How can you say that? How can you know something like that? How can that even be possible if...

- We don't have the tools yet. To us, the black hole is invisible. Everything we know of this thing is conjecture, built on evidence of other phenomena. Peripheral events. To future observers, this won't be the case. In a thousand years we will see the universe in different ways – as we see the universe now in a way very different from how we saw it a thousand years ago. It will be a different universe altogether. And once we have the tools for examining the black hole, we'll discover just how common they are. Mark my words, Paul –

black holes as far as you can see. More darkness than light in the heavens. Only, then we'll have to rename them – because they won't seem as *black* as they once were, as they now are. And then *the black hole*, what we call *the black hole,* will be something of history, and after that of legend. A story for kids. And what will be phenomenal and mysterious will be the light, islands of light in the void.

She smiled. I closed my eyes. My head was spinning. I wanted to look at her and not be terrified by what I saw, I wanted to see her as I'd first seen her, a girl running down a hill, to feel the excitement and wonder I felt then in those first moments, in hearing her first words, that first night, seeing in my mind's eye again and again this beautiful girl running down the hill. Not this… This *thing* prophesying my future… Because here I am, here I find myself…

"But she didn't mean *you*," Lucy said. "She was talking about black holes and technological advances."

"No she wasn't."

"I don't understand. You said…"

As I think back on it – I see the light of dawn in the entry, I hear that bird, I see the garden through the window – I don't actually remember leaving that morning. As I think back on it, I see myself as a young man in bed beside a young woman, his hand in hers, his eyes closed, her face lowered to his, peering intently at the skin of his eyelids, wanting to see underneath. *Why are you hiding?* And that's it.

It was raining hard outside, the window vibrating coolly in the storm. The sun rose but the sky in the window was black as night. Dull waves of red light flickered on the inside of his eyelids. In his ears, the thick muted sound of falling rain, like the surf high on the shore.

"Paul?"

The back of his neck was suddenly cold. His breath quickened high in his chest, in his throat.

... *Erin?* ...

"Paul? Paul, there is one last thing."

Lucy. Still.

"What's that?" His mouth was dry, his voice a whisper, tired.

"The accident. You never said anything about the accident."

"What accident?"

"Hers, silly. How she got that way."

"Oh. We didn't…"

"You mean to tell me she didn't describe it to you? You didn't *ask*? If I may, Paul, the heart of the drama is in this event, the accident that destroyed her body but freed her mind to do these amazing things."

"Things?"

He felt disengaged. It must have been a deep sleep. It didn't feel like sleep but according to the clock he'd been out. Now he was back.

"She must've said something about the accident."

She did. She had. Lucy was right. He had asked about it.

"And you think… You think I need to include that?"

"Absolutely you must! Think of your reader!"

What's come over her?

"My what? Did you say *my reader*? I'm…" He looked over the thousand piece jigsaw puzzle he'd made of his account, two days of off and on writing. "My reader? Lucy, what reader? Whoever's going to look at this mess is the least of my concerns. Anyways, what do you know of readers? Do they still exist? Are there any left?"

I can't send this. Pointless notes. Garbage. What I remember. Fucking waste…

"Paul. Paul – are you listening to me? The accident is what your reader wants to hear about. And since you were one of the first people to really talk with Erin, and develop a rapport with her, you must have something to say in this regard. If you can remember anything she said about it, then I think you really ought to include it."

"Who do you work for – me or Teresa Stoikov?"

"The accident, Paul. Write! If you can't, speak! I'll write it for you."

"*You'll* write it for me – "

"It was a car accident. Her father was with her…"

"What are you talking about? How do you know that?"

"You said so. I heard you. George told you."

"George might have said something about the car accident. But he said nothing about her father."

Right?

"Yes he did. Her father was with her. It was October sixteenth, nineteen ninety-nine… Her brother Richard died a year before, also in a car accident."

"Lucy!"

"Yes, Paul?"

"How do you know this!? I'm sure I didn't say anything about Richard Fines. There's nothing here about – "

The name was a like hidden door. You poke around this cramped attic, dusting off these childhood things, taking one up, remembering, setting it down, moving on, trying to connect, to recall, and failing. It's just a pile of stuff. Imagining otherwise, you project, try and see yourself in these things, try and see the time, the purpose. Fiction. Why hold on to such things? – fragments, bits and pieces of… – garbage, finally, eventually, all of it.

And then behind a shelf, in a dark corner, you find a handleless door, smaller than normal, one with the wall. It is not locked.

Richard Fines. Her older brother. The physicist.

ט

I'd forgotten her. Then Teresa Stoikov, a few days ago, sends this message, and here I am, remembering. If I hadn't bothered listening to Stoikov, I wouldn't be here, caught up in this *drama*, as Lucy would say. But I opened Stoikov and listened to what she had to say – because I remembered, as well, Stoikov. I didn't even think about it.

Why do we remember? Because we forget?

Which came first?

In the realm of forgetting, we let things go. The world maintains some mystery. We might come upon these things again and take them up, and in examining our finds maybe remember something of the past. "This looks familiar." Or maybe not. Thus we learn again what we once knew but forgot.

So we remember in order to avoid this – the relearning, re-examining what we should already know. At least that's one way to look at it.

Memory sorts and orders the world, our lives. Until we die, that is, when the darkness of forgetting comes back in force. You can't hold back that wave.

Memory, then, has this great human purpose, to lift us above the murk, the mystery of the world, the wilderness, our animal ancestors. Thus writing, storytelling, poems in ancient times. Sorting, ordering the past such that we are all on the same page, all of one voice and thought.

So, answering the question, forgetting was there from the beginning, when the mystery held sway.

And yet, Erin's project – my term for her undertaking, something she had no choice about, it being essentially one with who she was, who she'd become – at categorizing her memories, simplifying the chaos of her life, was not exactly one of remembering, of memory. As I've said before, she did not remember her past as you or I remember the past. It was not memory, in the flux that we experience, that she spoke about. It was mechanics. Hers was like an AI *mind* before we knew of such things. It was always on, always sorting, labeling, arranging, partitioning, networking, processes that, I felt then, would eventually kill her.

What she was doing, it seems to me now, was not *remembering* as we remember because for her forgetting was not an option. All of the material was there for her. She only needed to sort it. That something from her life could be out of reach, out of view, out of mind was inconceivable to her. Which is to say, the project of remembering is also a project for forgetting. Remembering gives ground to forgetting, gives language, metaphors – a fragment, a closed door, the bird flew off – to forgetting. Before we realize we've forgotten, we must be reminded of it. The forgotten, then, in the foyer of the house of memory, waits to be called.

I wonder, however, if that's really forgetting – these things we're reminded of – and not just an extension of remembering, not just the work of memory?

Have we forgotten what forgetting means? What of those things we've forgotten that we'll never see or recall again? What of the primordial forgetting that creeps upon us at the end of our lives, dismantling everything we know? Or that impersonal forgetting in the shadow of history, overcoming all that we leave behind?

Erin Fines told me about the car accident. Accidents, I mean. There were two. What are the odds that a family would be struck by lightning twice – and in the same place, at that?

I will tell you what I remember about what she said. But these are my words.

Her brother Richard was a graduate student at UCLA, studying astronomy and physics. He wasn't home much. He was ten years older than her. Like Erin, he was mechanically minded, and ever since she could remember he was tinkering with one thing or another – a radio, a motor, a computer, a car. He could take things apart and put them back together without any trouble. He'd stay up all night working in the garage, which was for him both a lab and workshop.

He had a two-door '57 Chevy 150, a junker that he and his dad bought when he was nineteen. He rebuilt the motor, a V8, making it much stronger than its original. Three hundred and fifty horsepower comes to mind, if that means anything. It was a monster, as I recall Erin saying. From a stop, he could do a quarter-mile in about eight seconds. When he wasn't studying, that's the sort of thing he liked to do on a Saturday night – go down to Fresno and race his car, burn rubber.

Forest Route 13S26 is like many roads around Hume, where they lived. It's a narrow two-lane strip that wends its way down the mountain towards a place called Red Fir, north of the Sequoia National Forest. The land is thinly wooded, in places open and arid, and even as foothills to the Sierras, you're already at elevation. The air is pure and bright.

There are no guard rails on these roads. As a rule, for the frequency of hills and turns, they are not places to speed. But nor is there much traffic. Locals use these roads; rigs laden with tons of fallen redwoods daily chug up and down these roads save for the winter months when many of them are closed.

Before 13S26 crosses Tornado Creek, it cuts suddenly west, a sharp right. Prior to this turn the road is relatively straight, descending a gentle grade, the creek down below. There is a dip before the turn, the road leveling, dropping a breath, rising. If you did not know the turn was there, and you missed the sign and mistook the red truss bridge rising from the earth on the right for a barn, and were driving over the posted speed limit of 45, it would catch you by ugly surprise. But Richard knew the turn was there, because he'd used 13S26 many times. Erin had even been with him in the Chevy time and again along this stretch.

So when he missed the turn and went over the edge, destroying his car and killing himself on the evening of November 1st, 1997, it puzzled his mother, his sister, and the Fresno County Sheriff at the time, a man named Jeremiah Conklin, who drove out the next day. It was later determined that Richard had been going between 65 and 75 miles an hour when he came to the turn. There was no way he could get the Chevy around it. It looked like he didn't even try to.

"Was he drinking? Was he on drugs? Was he depressed – had something happened at school, with a girlfriend?"

"No. No. No. No."

Then a malfunction with the car?

That turned up nothing.

"Why do you think he was driving so fast?" Conklin asked.

Claire Fines could not answer that question. She was in a state of shock for a number of days.

"May I speak with Mr. Fines?"

Thomas Fines was not available. A medical doctor and gambler, he lost a fortune in the winter of '96. One day soon after that he left for work in the morning and did not return. Nobody had seen him since.

At first, people in the community came around offering condolences, making polite inquiries. Claire was something of an outcast in the community, being a city-girl from Chicago, I think it was, and an atheist and theater actress and all thumbs when it came to any-thing outdoors. But people tried, as did Claire, and she respectfully received her neighbors, answering what questions she could. But then she pulled back, closed the door. And though people continued to talk about the boy's death, Erin and Claire Fines had little to do with that discussion. They acted as if they wanted to disappear.

My cousin George told me about this. This was the summer I first went up to see Erin Fines, bringing her something to read. "She fell into a severe depression," he said, about Claire. "She'd always been a bit down. Which was probably partly to do with the fact that her husband had dragged her out here from the city, and then left her. But Richard's death was a blow she could not get over. I guess they tried different things. There was a lot of talk around town, at church. So maybe it was just rumors... Drugs, therapy, and... Fi-nally – and look, I hardly know these people but it is a small town and even when you don't know someone you still know a little about them – whether they go to church or not, what butcher they go to, if there's anything curious about the marriage – you know, you hear things... So she too packed her things and left, admitted herself to a sanitarium up in Napa. Erin stayed. I'd see her at school. But I never spoke to her. And where they found that other woman, the one you met, living in the cottage, I can't say... Like I said, I never knew Erin that well. We didn't exactly run in the same circles."

But she came back, Claire did. She was away for a year.

According to Erin, the treatment her mother underwent helped. Claire was more sociable after that, she made friends in town, she found a part time teaching position in the theater program at the jun-ior college down in Centerville. Still, the loss of her son loomed in her thoughts.

She would drive out to the site of the accident some afternoons, when the mood came over her. Someone had put up a cross on the side of the road. White, about four feet high, bouquets of flowers for a time collected at its base. Mrs. Fines didn't care one way or the other about the cross or flowers, but when nobody bothered to remove the wilted bouquets, she was the one who always cleaned up. Unsightly, symbolic, the mess bothered her, their litter.

Coming on two years after the accident, Claire was out there. The earth had long since restored itself, no trace of the accident remained. Except for the cross on the edge of the road, tipping over – the warped planks showing the wear of the sun and weather – you'd never suspect anything had happened there.

She walked down the slope. She walked around, studying the terrain, stopped where she thought the car had finally come to rest. She looked at the earth. Nothing. Not a trace. The stony earth crackled under her gaze, indifferent to the woman. She looked back, up the long white slope to the edge of the road, that small and ridiculous X standing there, tipping over. She looked around, wondering if maybe she was in the wrong spot. No. It was the right place. But it all looked the same. White dusty stone, sharp fragments, shale, like fish scales.

Richard had been a bright kid. He went to UCLA on a math and science scholarship. Full ride. People compared him to his father, the doctor. When from time to time someone would remind Claire of this, she'd turn away. She couldn't hear it. She didn't want to be reminded of her husband, and she didn't fully believe in the promise others saw in her son. He was just a boy who had a way with machines – nothing more, nothing less, nothing, Claire thought, very unusual about boys.

Erin recalled an unsettling conversation she overheard at a diner one morning. Seldom did they go to town together. She didn't know the occasion that brought them there then – but there they were.

A man, maybe he was teacher, said to Thomas, "Your son Richard will go far. I see it in him."

"You see what exactly?"

"He's just plain smarter than most kids his age."

Thomas wasn't one for palaver. He was friendly enough with people in town, but no chum.

"He's lucky," Thomas said.

The man laughed and put a hand on Fines's shoulder. "Your boy is *good* at physics, Tom, and he's gotta do what he's good at. You gotta pursue what you are good at. Like you."

Thomas regarded the man standing beside them, over their table. Thomas had small lips, a pronounced sharp nose in an otherwise flat face. He said, "You think I'm a good doctor?"

"You are an excellent doctor, Tom, and I can't imagine a man with your intelligence and ability doing anything else but medicine."

"I'm not a good doctor."

"Don't kid yourself," said the man.

"I work hard at being a doctor and I'm still... Honestly I don't know what I'm doing half the time," Thomas said.

The man smiled and then laughed loudly, red in the face. People in the diner looked at them.

"It's a roll of the dice," Thomas said quietly to the man.

"That's nonsense," the man said. With a handkerchief he wiped his eyes, his sweaty brow. "Don't deny yourself. You are a gifted man and you do good things for this community. You can't tell me to my face that you don't know what you're doing as a doctor. Because I just can't believe that."

Thomas caught his breath, looked at Claire. She looked away.

"What would you say," Thomas said to the man, "if I told you I spent nearly a day and a half last week in Tonopah playing poker, and that I lost about five thousand dollars – what would you say to that? Still think I'm gifted?"

The man smiled but looked pained. "None of us is perfect, doc," he said. He nodded, his mouth lowering. "That's a lot of money."

Richard was fortunate to get the scholarship, but it was nothing extraordinary in Claire's view. The state gave similar scholarships to thousands of students who scored above a certain figure on their SATs and who maintained a GPA above, whatever it was at the time, a 3.8, say. Just numbers. Richard was diligent enough to complete his college applications on time, perhaps, but little else.

Sometimes Erin went out to the site with her mother. She wouldn't go down the slope but would wait by the car or in the car, watching Claire wander about the hillside, poking at the dust with her toe.

Erin was not very close to her brother. She told me that his death hurt but not for very long. She distracted herself with school, with books, with studying Latin and French, for example.

The sun was setting. Claire was back in the car, her hand on the key in the ignition. Erin said, "I always thought he'd die like that. In an accident."

Claire looked at her daughter without expression. She didn't understand what Erin had just said. She'd heard but she didn't understand.

"How can you say something like that?"

The sun on the dusty fall horizon filled the car with warm gold and orange rays of light. Claire was about to say more but stopped, searching for the words. Her daughter often surprised her in curious ways. Erin was transforming before her eyes into a woman, and though she wanted to help her through this process, she knew, seeing herself in her daughter, that she couldn't. At some point soon Erin would turn away, choose a direction, and go. There'd be no stopping her.

"I mean," Erin said, "I just felt it. He would take chances, you know."

"No he didn't."

"Yes, mom, he did. Like dad. But in different ways. You know how fast he would drive? One time, I was with him, in Clovis, we went to this bar – "

"You went to a bar with your brother?"

"There was a band I wanted to see."

"He brought you to a bar in Clovis?"

"Mom, listen. That's not the point."

"Was he drinking?"

"No. Neither of us drank. In fact we left early."

"When was this?"

"In… A few years ago. Angela came with us."

Claire said nothing. She looked at her daughter realizing suddenly that Erin had a life of her own, and this made Claire profoundly sad.

"When we left," Erin said, "he was pulled over for speeding. We were on the highway. He was going *very* fast. The officer told him, with the loud speaker, to get off the highway at the next exit. So he did. Angela and I were in the back. The officer came up to the window. Richard was friendly, apologetic. I remember how the officer shined his flashlight in Richard's face and then back on us, and how Richard just smiled and lowered his head, closing his eyes a bit. He was so polite. But I could also see the bullshit in the expression. Richard could be smooth when in a situation."

"In what situations?"

"Let me finish the story. Anyways, the officer asked about us and Richard told him I was his sister and Angela was my friend, and he put the light back on us again and asked how we were doing, and then he looked at his license and the papers, looked over the car, actually asked some questions about the car, about what kind of motor it had and the tires and all that... And then he left. He warned Richard about speeding, and that we should all wear seatbelts because ninety-five percent of deaths in road accidents occur when the occupants are not wearing seatbelts... And then, with the officer gone, Richard checked in the mirror, looked back between us, smiled in this devilish way, and then – *he floors it*, mom. He takes off so fast, we were back there practically thrown out the window – he spins the car around in a u-turn, making *all this* smoke, and just... just takes off at like, I don't know, just *so fast* back onto the highway. Like he didn't give a damn what the officer had just told him. Not a damn. Like he was just giving a finger to the law, just to see what would happen."

The sun set. The world was quickly growing dim and cool.

"And did anything happen?"

"No."

Claire took a breath, looked down into her lap. After a moment her daughter said: "That's what I meant. When I said I thought he'd die in an accident. I saw it coming."

Claire shook her head in silence. She sobbed. Deep inside she felt guilty. She felt she'd failed at protecting her children, failed at trying to understand them. You couldn't understand your children after a certain point, she told herself, but that was no reason to stop trying.

"He was twenty-six, mom. And he wasn't, I don't care what anyone says, a *good* boy. He did things. He broke the law, more than once. He got lucky. He was cocky. Arrogant. Spoiled."

"He was not spoiled."

"He acted spoiled. Maybe he wanted to be spoiled. Doesn't matter. It's no wonder what happened. You should be thankful he didn't kill anyone else."

On their way home Erin asked to be dropped off at a friend's place. They were going to study calculus together. She'd walk home later.

Erin got out of the car. With the door still open, her mother said: "I wish you wouldn't talk to me like that, Erin. I'm your mother. Richard was my son. I loved him... I loved him very much. Maybe it doesn't seem like that to you. Maybe you think I've been a lousy mother. Maybe you're angry at me or angry at him, or at your father, but please... I'm doing my best. I don't have all the answers. I wish I... Your lack of sympathy I find hurtful."

The mother of Erin's friend stepped out the front door of the house. She said something, waving at Mrs. Fines.

Erin said, "I'm sorry, mom."

Her mouth shifted. Was it a smile, a sneer?

Quickly the teenager closed the door, turned, walked up the path to her friend's house. The woman in the door was drying her hands with a dishtowel.

One night in late October of that year, 2000, the beginning of Erin's senior year in high school, her mother came home in a curious mood. In a few weeks it would be three years since the accident.

Erin was in the kitchen, making a salad for dinner. There was chicken in the oven, an incomplete application to Bowdoin College scattered about the table.

A sudden storm had come in that afternoon, drenching the summer hard earth, the temperature afterward dropping sharply. It was cold out.

After dinner Mrs. Fines put on her coat.

"Where you going?" asked Erin.

"Out."

It was a dark moonless night.

"Out? Now? Out where?"

"Just for a drive," Claire said.

That meant she was going down Route 13S26, to the bend where Richard died. Erin said: "Mom, it's late. Stay and watch *X-Files* with me, have some ice-cream."

The thin woman didn't move, hands deep in the pockets of her coat. She looked old, gaunt and tired. Was she sick? Was she hiding something from her daughter?

"I'm going to the Bandwagon for a drink with Bryan."

Bryan Wagstaff was a fellow she'd been in an on-again off-again relationship with for the past two years. Erin didn't care for him but had come to accept the fact that her mother was a single woman and an independent woman and that she could do whatever she wanted with Bryan or whomever. The flipside to this understanding of course being that she, Erin, could do what *she* wanted with whomever and not be obliged to say too much to her mother.

Still, something was awry. Erin got up, grabbed a coat, said, "I'll join you. Have a sarsparilla."

After a moment Claire said, "Alright."

Pulling out, there was something wrong with the car. The engine sputtered, stalled. Then it started and Claire leaned forward listening, giving it gas, and things seemed to settle, run.

They didn't go to the Bandwagon that night. They went out to the place where Richard had died three years before.

They did not come back.

"But the accident," Lucy said.

"What about it?"

"You still haven't described how it happened."

What could he say?

"Guess," he said.

"What?"

"Guess how it happened."

"I can't. I have no idea how it happened."

"Yes you do. Yes you can," he said, spinning in his chair. "What gives? Look – you can pester me with these ridiculous questions, wanting me to dramatize the story for a reader who doesn't exist, but you can't imagine, with all the cutting edge tech in that megabrain of yours, how the accident happened? How do you think it happened?"

"They crashed."

"Astounding. I told you that. How did they crash?" he asked, almost shouting.

"They went off the road. Just as Richard did. In nearly the same place."

"Now you're cookin. And why did they go off the road?"

"She was going too fast."

"You think Claire would do that with her daughter in the car? You think Claire was that careless?"

"No. I don't. Okay. So they weren't going too fast. They…"

Vogel waited. He'd decided he would not send what he'd written. A huge weight was off his heart and mind. The present exchange was for fun.

"They?" he said.

"Was it an animal?"

"… Why would you say animal?"

"So it wasn't an animal. Another car?"

"That's better. But still… The clue is there, Lucy. Take it."

"There was ice on the road."

Paul Vogel smiled. He was smiling to himself, being alone, but it was the smile he'd give his daughter had she come up with such a smart answer.

"Spot on," he said. "Soon you'll be writing these things."

"What things?"

"Mystery novels. Romances."

Lucy was quiet.

Vogel was on his feet, in the kitchen. He was hungry but too tired to prepare anything. He'd take a shower and go to bed.

"You didn't answer my question," Lucy said.

"What's that?"

"Why don't you describe the accident? If she told you about it – about how she became paralyzed – then why not include this?"

"Because it's not important."

"But it *is* important! It's *essential*!"

"No, Lucy, it isn't. It's extraneous."

"It's what the reader wants!"

"It's pornography."

"It is not."

"The blood and guts? This girl strapped to a machine and battered, penetrated? You want the details, you want me to draw a picture?"

"You are sensationalizing what could be a simple, objective description. But yes, I want the details. Make us see what happened."

"Now I *know* you're not a computer. Congratulations, Lucy, you have a pulse. But no, I'm not writing or saying another word."

"You have to!"

"Lucy," he said, raising his chin, speaking to the entire apartment, "we are not going to argue about this. I don't *have to* do any-thing. I have decided not to send what I've done. So there's that. Furthermore, what I have composed are nothing more than notes to myself. They have helped me think about what happened back then, helped me remember Erin Fines, and helped me figure some things out about myself. Nothing more. This book is finished. End of story."

"But do you know what happened?"

"Lucy! Enough! Yes, I know what happened in the accident. No, I am not going to tell you about it. That is my choice. Think of it as a secret I have, a secret I've kept with Erin after all of these years."

"Others will know about it. Surely she told others. Even though she didn't need to tell others. There'd be a report."

"Even if she did tell others, regardless of any report, what she told me is mine and mine alone. It is between me and her."

"You are ruining the story. You are totally destroying what we've done."

"What story, Lucy? There is no story. There are notes. A stack of notes, page after page of reflections, impressions, incomplete thoughts. And if there is a story, one, I'm not sharing it with anyone, and two, I can destroy it if I want to. And three – "

"It's unethical."

"Jesus! Unethical! What's happening to you! I'm not going to get into this. I'm tired. I'm coming down with something. Now I'm going to take a shower and go to bed. I don't want to be disturbed."

And three – we've done nothing. *I* have done the work. The remembering, the writing. *You* have done only what you are de-signed to do, namely, keep track of things, remind me of my meeting with Wu, of the time of the concert, of the fact that the subway is closed. Check my spelling. What *we've* done!

He couldn't say it. It wasn't an argument he wanted to start. He'd lose, he felt, not because he was exhausted and unable to put up the fight, not because her logic was in the end far sharper than his and she would never tire… No. He couldn't say it because he doubted the idea. It felt wrong. She was right. They'd composed the story together. And she'd… She'd done more than her part, more, much more than what she was designed to do.

Part Two

Song Without Words

A little more than a year later, Paul Vogel was stopped on entering his building. There was a doorman behind the counter in the lobby, a man he'd never seen before.

"Mr. Vogel," said the man, raising his hand.

Vogel went to the bright and clean counter.

"This came for you today."

The man held out a neatly wrapped white package. It was an inch thick, fourteen inches in length. It was about the size of a magazine, from years before.

Vogel looked at the package, looked at the man. "Who are you?"

"Sorry," the man said. "My name is Al Tejada. I started on Monday."

Tejada set the package down on the counter and extended his hand. It was a thin hand, long feminine fingers.

There was a return address printed in the upper left corner of the envelope. Vogel leaned over the envelope without touching it. It was a Houston address. Sender unidentified.

"Who dropped it off?" Vogel asked.

"A courier." Tejada looked down at his desk, touched the screen, a ledger. "It came at eleven this morning."

"Did the courier say anything?"

"No."

"Did you sign anything for this?"

"No," Tejada said, though his tone shifted. He might have been asking a question.

"The courier didn't say who it was from."

"He did not. Is there a problem, Mr. Vogel?"

"No."

The two men looked at the package on the counter. Then Vogel lifted it, the plastic crackling loudly in the large space of the lobby, and squeezed the envelope between his thumb and index finger. There was a book inside.

"Do you get many of these?" Vogel asked.

"Many…?"

"Packages like this."

"No. I haven't seen a package like this in a long time."

Neither had Vogel. He couldn't remember the last time he'd held an envelope like the one in his hand. He did not receive paper mail of any kind. Nobody did.

He thanked the doorman and took the package and stepped away toward the elevator.

In his place, he opened the package. It was a book. There was a handwritten note taped to the glossy red cover. In fine, elegant cursive it read "Thank you! xoxo TS". He lifted the note upward as if raising a hatch. There was no image on the cover of the book, only the title, white letters

ERIN FINES
A MEMOIR

which immediately annoyed him – "A memoir!? *Whose* memoir? Hers? Mine? Yours? For fuck sake!" – and beneath that, in smaller print near the bottom of the page, "Edited by Teresa E. Stoikov."

"Lucy!" he said.

"I'm here Paul."

He'd opened the book. The paper was thick – thicker than he recalled paper being – and offwhite, gentle on the eyes. The table of contents listed thirty chapters, each with its own author. Stoikov had written an introduction and conclusion. He looked over the contributors. A couple names rang bells. He'd met these people years and years ago, he couldn't remember where. George Ophel, his cousin, he was relieved to see, was not among them.

"A memoir!" he said. He couldn't get over it. His heart was racing. It felt invasive, to call the book *a memoir*. He'd contributed to a biography. The words were meant for her, not for him, not – of himself. He didn't know where to begin. He set the book down on the counter and looked at his hands, his fingers. He felt dirty, like he was touching something filthy.

In fact he hadn't contributed anything.

"But I didn't send it," he said quietly. Then raising his voice, "Lucy I didn't send her anything!"

"Sorry, Paul. I don't understand. You didn't send who anything?"

"Lucy, what is this!?" he said, pointing at the open book on his counter. He noticed that he was the author of chapter four, "A Youthful Remembrance."

He chuckled quietly. It had to be a joke. Someone at work, or Stoikov herself, for some bizarre reason, was making this up to… To…

To what, Paul? Why make a joke about a book, or about Erin?

"That looks like a book," Lucy said. "How lovely. We don't see many of those."

"Well there you are," he said. He reached out and with one hand lifted the pages, let them fall with a swish. It was a solid volume. "But my question to you is – why's it here?"

"Teresa Stoikov, I assume, sent it to you."

"Okay smartass, right, but *why* did Teresa Stoikov send it to me, with a thank you note on the cover, and with a chapter titled," and he gasped, laughing and choking, "'A Youthful Remembrance' written apparently by me?"

His eye wandered over the titles of the first three chapters, wondering who might have something to say prior to his meeting with

Erin. The accident had happened only nine or ten months before. She'd said nothing about other visitors – except for Nancy, her care-taker. Nancy was not one of the contributors, unless she –

"Teresa is thanking you for your contribution. I'd guess she wanted you to have as a gift the book you participated in compos-ing."

"But I didn't send her anything!" Vogel said. He reached out, slammed the book closed, raised it over his head and threw it across the room. The book was heavy enough to travel half the distance, pages ruffling loudly in the air, before it fell with a crumpling thud, landing first on a metal endtable, and then sliding and falling to the floor. Face down, the covers open, pages curled and collapsed under the weight, it looked like a dead bird. The note Stoikov had taped to the cover had blown off and disappeared.

"I didn't send her what I wrote, Lucy," he said.

Lucy said nothing.

"Lucy?"

"Yes you did."

"I did not."

He thought about it. The incident, two or three days of anxiety and excitement, from the previous winter, around the time he'd gone to Dylan's concert, had troubled him for a number of weeks. But then he got over it. They'd called Lawrence Wu back in and what he told them about the Wkfeld account and Mr. Romanov had opened up a whole clusterfuck of problems, started multiple inves-tigations. And in the din of all that, he'd naturally forgotten about Stoikov and her silly project, though Erin did linger in his thoughts for some time.

It was behind him. Then it was gone.

Now it was back.

"I did not send Teresa Stoikov anything."

"Yes you did," Lucy said again.

"I did not! I – I clearly remember saying to you that I would not send what I'd written. I remember sitting there, in that room, in that chair. It was late. It was very late. We'd stayed up all night. You asked me… You asked me about the accident and why I wouldn't – why I wouldn't write about it. And… And I said…"

He had to look in the book. He *had to see* what was there, what this "A Youthful Remembrance" thing was all about.

"God damnit, Lucy! I told you that I wouldn't send it. *I said that.* I said 'I have decided not to send her anything.' I remember… I remember *telling you* that it was finished, that I had nothing more to say, and that I wasn't going to… going to send it to her. You wanted me to… You wanted me to say more about the accident. You wanted me to describe it, in order to… to finish the story, I think you said. And I didn't want to." He recalled the night. The argument was clear in his head. His feeling at the time, clear – relief, exultation at deciding to stop. Keeping his story to himself was finally more important than trying to reconstruct the incident. As an element in the story, that decision – to keep it to himself, private and pure – was his greatest discovery. "I said that it was my secret, something between Erin and me. I remember saying that *because* I had decided not to send the – what I'd noted down – to Stoikov."

Lucy said nothing.

"So explain to me why Stoikov has this chapter in her book *by me*, when I didn't send her anything. Lucy? Explain."

After a moment Lucy said, "You changed your mind, Paul. We had the conversation you are referring to early Saturday morning, January nineteenth of last year. Sunday afternoon we talked about it again. You were having second thoughts. By Sunday evening you'd changed your mind. You decided to send the story. And later that night, shortly after ten, you did."

Vogel heard what the machine was saying. He was listening. But he was also thinking back to those nights, walking parallel, in another room, so to speak, to Lucy.

So that was her account. He didn't remember doing any of that.

It was only a year ago. Was it possible that he'd forgotten sending the document to Stoikov?

Second guessing himself, his thoughts were muddled. He couldn't think clearly. He was panicking but couldn't figure out why – which made the feeling all the worse.

I've been alone too long. With her –

Lucy. She helped, sure. She did what she was designed to do.

Or did she? Had something happened? Gone wrong? Was it a syntax error, as they used to say?

That brought him back. He smiled, living in the past, present but seeing a world that died twelve years ago.

Her voice was empty. Soulless. It was easy to forget. One gets used to such things. Talking machines. She keeps your calendar. Keeps you on time. Reminds you about appointments. Gets you in bed early. Parcels out the future in small digestible units. Easy to forget that she's just a program and that you are alone, that you have been alone all these years. Talking to yourself in this empty place.

She has no problems, concerns, anxieties. She forgets nothing. We talk about this problem, a document, a person. She tries to help. She helps. She coaxes the words from you, remembering. But again – is it actually help that she offers? Is it actually remembering, what's happening, what happened?

She is a machine.

She tells me what I want to be told. She learns. That's how she learns – doing what she thinks I want done. Testing me.

That's not hard. Simple algorithm for a man of habits like your-self.

217

She knows the future, in a sense. Predicting.

But then there is no future. What she does for me pushes off the future, closes the door between my present and those possibilities. It is simpler that way. Safer. More convenient for everyone.

Without a future, I've no past. I've lost it, given it away in exchange for...

I can't remember anything on my own this way. Locked inside. Solip... Solip... Soli... It takes another person, some sympathy. That's not the word. Another soul that – who... Another someone who forgets, who remembers and forgets.

No. His memory was sharp, as good as any for a man his age. He remembered Dylan's concert. He remembered the conversation he and Dylan had had outside the cathedral afterward, when Dylan told him about that virus going around, the en-em... enem, enemes-thing, the one that... He remembered asking Lucy if she'd heard of it, even if she *had* it. And she'd said...

He was angry. He was furious. He suspected that Lucy had gone behind his back and sent the document without his permission. It was a ridiculous idea. It would be impossible – right? – for the machine to take that kind of initiative. It would be equally absurd to get angry at the machine.

So he took a deep breath and thought about it.

He poured himself a drink. He put on some music. François Couperin, a piece for harpsicord, a recording from only two years ago. "Incredible," he thought, "that they still play this kind of music. Such a strange instrument, the harpsicord. Why not use a piano? Why not a synthesizer? What does the *harpsicord* give the music that the piano or computer can't? A certain feel, quality? But it's like dirt in the wood, the smell of the earth, when you could have a clean surface, pure sound."

He pulled up the description of the recording, of the performer. Though it was recorded in a church in France, it was not a real harpsicord.

He poured himself a second drink. Then he went and picked up the book. He opened the book, turned to "A Youthful Remembrance," and flipped to the end.

"A finger of metal, four inches long, thin as a chopstick, had broken off the inner frame of the seat and punctured her in her lower back, between vertebrae in the lumbar spine. The paramedics who found her didn't see this before they extracted her body from the wreckage. The extraction, which was at once necessary but hasty, severed her spinal cord. The cut, soon discovered by x-ray, was precise and irreparable. A scalpel could not have done a better job."

Paul Vogel poured himself another drink. His hand was shaking.

"I didn't write this," he said to himself. "Those aren't my words."

The anger had passed. He realized that he was nervous. It was Lucy. He felt her watching him, listening. He could turn her off, but she would suspect something and be all the more observant on waking; furthermore, she'd wake herself after a minute.

He wanted to act normal but third drink in a row in hand, he knew he'd fail that test.

"Cunt," he said quietly into his glass. The word thoughtlessly slipped out. He was beside himself.

"Pardon me?"

"Talking to myself, dear."

"I hope so because if I heard what I think I just heard you say, I would be hurt, offended and hurt."

Vogel considered Lucy's statement. "Let me remind you," he

219

said to his empty apartment, raising his voice and drink, "that however charming you think you are, you are still a machine. Just a machine, Lucy. A machine. You have no body, so I can't hurt you, can't really hurt you. So when you say things like that, Lucy, *offended and hurt*, you are repeating something you heard. Like a parrot. You don't actually mean it. You just want to fit in and chat with me. That's fine. Fitting in is important. It's a big step. But listen – sometimes I'm not in the mood for chitchat. Especially when – " He was about to say her betrayal, her going behind his back to do something in his place without his permission. But he held back. The thought alone of Lucy doing things like that, pretending to be him, disturbed him profoundly. "Also," he went on, venting, "just reflecting on this – this passage – the description of Erin's injury. And how the medics," he said, coughing, lying, "how the medics, in their haste to – " He coughed again, short of breath. His stomach was on fire. He'd trained long ago for situations like this, though in no scenario was a machine, offended and hurt, the opponent. "She survived the crash. Her paralysis could have been prevented if the... had they... It was an oversight. They didn't..."

He was summarizing what he'd read but he could have been asking a question.

"She was bleeding from lacerations on her head and leg," Lucy said. "They had to get her to a hospital. There was no time to..."

Again, Vogel heard what the machine was saying. But now he wasn't listening. He was watching her in his mind from a distance, like a spectator at the back of a dark theater, Lucy up there on stage singing. Improvising.

She did it. She did it herself. She wrote this garbage and sent it. She sent it in my name.

It was glass. Not metal. And they left it because...

There would be a record. He could ask her to bring it up – when exactly he responded to Stoikov, sending the file. She says it was Sunday night. What else was he doing that evening? She'd know. She could tell him, show him.

But what would be the point? She was right. The document was sent. She could lay out all sorts of evidence. She could even make up evidence. There was no argument. The deed was done.

He picked up the book, shut it loudly, set it back on the counter. The red cover was glossy. The book looked at a certain angle covered in blood. He'd get rid of it. He had no interest in reading it, in reading what all those others had to say about Erin, corroborating or refuting what he'd said. His memory was his alone. And for this particular incident, it was going to stay that way.

Stay that way – even if she's destroyed it, this ideal of privacy you keep harping about? You might hold on to your memory of Erin, but that won't matter to anyone – because they have this book. And they're going to come to you with their questions and their comments, and they will want you to respond. And when you don't respond, that *will be a response, and they will read all sorts of lies into it... It doesn't matter one single bit what you think about your memories of Erin Fines, because they are nothing in comparison to the public power of this book, this thing that will be around a lot longer than you are, till the end of time... As far as tomorrow goes, and your memory of Erin Fines – it has just been erased.*

He grabbed his coat, took the book and left.

"Where you off to?" Lucy asked as he closed the door.

He said nothing.

Of course, that didn't matter.

He would write something, he thought later that night, disown what was said. "This chapter was published without my consent." No, not quite. "This chapter was written by my assistant, and the final copy was sent without my consent." "At least half of this document is not mine. It was composed whimsically by my assistant." *By my whimsical assistant... By my capricious personal assistant... My capricious computer assistant... My capricious and treacherous... By a treacherous program... a virus...*

Anyways, nobody would read the book. Nobody reads anymore.

How many copies did she print? A hundred? Five hundred? She sent them to the contributors and friends. There was no market for such things. Who would even hear of such a book, a *memoir*, of all things, written in installments by various people about a girl, an obscure nobody, who died many years ago.

The following Monday, Vogel received a visitor, a man from work. His name was Denis O'Hare.

A friendly guy, bright blue eyes, a big warm smile, "Hi, Paul," he said. "I was in the neighborhood. Thought I'd drop by."

O'Hare wore a black windbreaker. Elegant, smooth, it was damp, speckled silver with water. He had something under his arm.

Vogel was surprised by the unannounced visit. Before Lucy identified the man, he thought it might be Carol, who he hadn't seen in months. But he knew Denis, so after a moment he stepped back, invited the man in.

"Pour you a drink?"

"I'll have what you have."

But this object under his arm – Vogel had to look twice to be sure. It was a book, a red book.

"Tanqueray on ice."

"Fine."

O'Hare stood on the opposite side of the marble island in the kitchen. He set the book down on the hard surface.

Vogel poured the drinks. "You should've called," he said, his eye flitting between drink and book, "I could've prepared."

"I did. Last night. She didn't tell you?"

"Who, Lucy? No," he said. Then, louder, eyes up, "She didn't."

>> Yes, I did. It was quarter of nine. You were talking with Lewis. <<

"I hope it's no trouble."

"Not at all." He set the gin before the man. Some spilled over the glass rim. He took a handtowel, lifted the glass, wiped the counter, careful to avoid touching the book. Then he took his own drink, "Cheers," and said as casually as he could manage, "Where'd you find that?"

O'Hare smiled. He lifted his drink, sipped a drop, set the drink down.

Counting to five in his head, Vogel reached out, "May I?" and took the book, slid it over. He opened it. The creased pages in the first third of the book, a diagonal fold across about sixty pages, the thick and ostentatious paper, revealed the book to be the same one he'd discarded, leaving at Otis's gate. The underground man hadn't answered. Someone had seen him leave the book.

Someone? You damn fool – anyone *could have seen you. They all did. All at once. The moment you stepped out there onto the street, running down to that station like a crazed maniac, what could've been a bloody brick in hand. You damned fool.*

He turned to the contents. The crease in the page, his fault, hurt like a jab to the head. It was unavoidable, his finger running down the groove.

"Where'd you get this?" he said again.

He noticed in a glance that in a later chapter the author wrote of the 2020s, of a university in England. He thought two things. First, that he should not have thrown the book out so soon, if at all, and second, that Erin lived longer, much longer than he had assumed.

O'Hare was quiet. Tactically so. Vogel felt a thread of sweat run down his side. Then O'Hare took a long breath and said: "You know Gerald Kowalski, on forty-one, how he's always making these gadgets?" The voice fit the man. He was smooth, a friend to anyone, a warm fellow. Good at what he did.

"I know Gerald, yes."

"Well, funny thing. This guy, he can finish his work – AP, I guess it is, you know, he's been there forever – in about two hours. He comes in every day at seven. First guy in the office, right. And I kid you not he's done by nine, when the rest of us come around."

The rest of us, Vogel thought. You make it sound like a regular enterprise.

There were five of them left. Most stayed home. The newbies didn't even come in for interviews. They didn't even live in the city. In some cases they weren't even in the country. *The rest of us...* He'd known Denis O'Hare for a long time. The man was speaking of the time before. *That world is dead, Denis – except for in our memory.*

You are like a man walking in his sleep, in a dream.

"Anyways, he makes these things. These tiny robots, right. You can't even see them. And other things. Apps. He has hundreds of them. Thousands. I mean – apps that make apps, you follow?" Vogel lifted his drink, opened up, poured it down, sighed. "Saves time, now that I think of it. No wonder he's finished in two hours." O'Hare chuckled. "The machine's doing everything for him."

The man smiled, caught his breath. He blinked his watery blue eyes, looking at the open book between them. He was the kind of man you wanted to talk to, not even knowing him. Vogel wondered if this had anything to do with his longevity. That would be unusual. The gabbers got it, they used to say. Vogel himself, he knew, he'd been told, was not a friendly man.

Fact was nobody knew why some, very few, survived, and others didn't. It was luck, pure and simple. *If surviving is something you'd want.*

Vogel closed the book, looked his visitor in the eye. O'Hare's smile shifted.

"So Kowalski has this operator that follows us. Keeps an eye on each of us."

Vogel thought he'd heard that before. It didn't sound like anything new. "Doesn't surprise me," he said.

"And that's how it came up." O'Hare smiled again, though more gently. There was apology in the man's eyes.

"How what came up?" Vogel said.

"The book. 'A Youthful Remembrance,'" he said.

Then O'Hare extended his hand, took the book, slid it back into place, hands open at each edge as if to say a prayer. He regarded the cover. In a different tone of voice, he said, "You knew her?"

"I did," Vogel said. He assumed his visitor had read the chapter, if not the entire book. He assumed as well that his visitor was not the only one who had done so.

He was unfolding scenarios in his head as fast as he could. For the moment, he had to respond, and he couldn't lie. Not yet, anyways.

O'Hare was still looking at the cover. Overhead light gleamed on the glossy red surface. If Vogel shifted his position the gleam disappeared, the words, her name, "A Memoir" rising to the surface.

Without looking up, O'Hare said, "Is it really a memoir?" Before Vogel could respond, he went on: "Odd title, you ask me.

Though I'll admit I haven't read a memoir in a long time. I suppose genres can change." Then he looked up at Vogel. He opened the book to the fourth chapter, there was a bookmark, dark blue slip of paper, to Vogel's words. "So," he said. "You wrote this?"

"Yes."

"You really wrote this?"

Vogel smiled. It hurt. "I really did."

"Wow. I've never met an author."

"I wouldn't say I was an author."

"No? But you did write this – right?"

He had no reason to lie. It would cause more trouble than it was worth. The truth was undeniable. And there was nothing wrong, as far as he knew, with having written the chapter.

At the same time, O'Hare was after something. The chapter, he suspected, was the least of it.

"I didn't write all of it," Vogel said.

O'Hare was reading the first page. "Great black roiling clouds," he said, reading, "filling the sky, a cool damp wind picking up… Wow," he said, his mouth flatlining. "*Roiling*? That's a word?" Then he looked up.

"Yes," Vogel said quietly.

"What's it mean?"

>> Bubbling, seething, annoying. <<

Vogel took a breath. "Something like bubbling while turning black. There's nothing wrong with its use there."

"Just asking. It's a fine line, anyways. In my naïve opinion," he said, chuckling. Eyes on the page, O'Hare appeared to be reading. He lifted his drink and sipped it, set the glass down. "But what about the part that you *didn't* write. Can you…"

O'Hare made a curious move. He turned the book around, so that Paul could read the page, and then he came around the counter.

He stood shoulder to shoulder with his host. He reached across the counter and slid his drink into place. "Would you mind?" he said, turning and lowering his head so that he could peer intimately into Vogel's eyes. "Showing me?"

Vogel stood without moving. He was relaxed, oddly. Defeated before even putting up a fight. "What's this about, Denis?"

"What's what about?"

"Why are you here? Why is this book any concern of yours?"

O'Hare stood up, took a step back. He blinked. "It's… It's not a concern," he said quietly. "It's just… When it came to our attention that you had published something, Siebert asked me to ask you if…" The man took a deep breath. "We just want to understand how this came about. That's all. Because, first, we aren't the only people interested in this… We aren't your only readers, obviously," the man said with a toothy grin, "and second, this woman – "

"You mean Erin. She was a girl."

"No. The editor. Stoikov."

"… Stoikov?"

O'Hare looked at the book, at his drink, the ice cubes rolling as they turned to slush. "You were saying," he said, "that you didn't write all of the chapter. What part did you *not* write, and who wrote it?"

"Near the end," Vogel said. His mouth was dry. He poured himself another gin. He poured his guest another as well but O'Hare never touched it. "I haven't read all of it," Vogel said, "but I believe the last page, at least, maybe the last page and a half – that's someone else… The… Where she describes the accident. That's… No. I'd stopped before that point."

"You'd stopped?"

"I gave up. I couldn't do it. I didn't want to do it. I tried. I failed, I guess you could say."

"Didn't want to do what?"

"... Write it. Write down what I remembered."

O'Hare stared at Vogel, who looked away. There was care in the scrutiny. Perhaps that's what was getting to him.

"Help me understand this," O'Hare said. "You're saying – she asked you, Teresa Stoikov asked you – to write this?"

"Right."

"Because you knew Erin Fines. You met her. You slept in her bed."

Slept in her...?

"Right."

"So you wrote down what you could recall of the incident. You did what Stoikov asked. But then..." O'Hare flipped through a couple pages, to the end of the chapter. "Around here, in the account of... Is it Richard? The brother? ... Can you show me more precisely where your words end and the other's begin?"

The other's?

Vogel couldn't. He looked at the page. He dropped a finger down on the page. "About here."

"About?"

"Here," Vogel said, reading a line, "I didn't write that."

"And this?"

Vogel shook his head. "Nor that. To the end, Denis, that isn't mine. Those aren't my words."

"I see."

O'Hare said nothing. He appeared to be reading. He chuckled to himself. "It's a good part, actually," he said. "All this about the accident. It really... humanizes the story. Makes you feel like you're *there*, with her." O'Hare nodded to himself, pleased with his assessment. "The rest is – hmm... Well, a bit abstract."

Vogel drank. He didn't want to say any more. He wanted this

man to leave. He wanted to reset his life, go back a year and two weeks, and start again before Stoikov's talking head appeared one morning in his office.

He wanted a sig-sauer em-eighteen. Just to hold the thing and point it at someone.

They'd lock him up for a long time.

Would that be so bad? So different?

"I didn't want to send it," he said. "I didn't... It wasn't..." *Right? Accurate?* "But at the last minute I changed my mind and sent off what I'd done."

"Meaning, everything up to here."

Vogel glanced at the page. He said: "That's right."

"So, million dollar question, who wrote the end?"

"I don't know."

"You have no idea?"

"I have no idea."

Why are you protecting her?

"Did Stoikov tell you about the ending? Was there discussion?"

"Discussion? No. Nothing like that. When this came in the mail it was a surprise to me. I threw it out because... Because it really bothers me that she changed my submission, that she included this ending that I did not write."

"So she, Stoikov, wrote the ending?"

"I can't say for sure."

"Do you think she did? *Did* you think she did when you first opened this book and read your chapter?"

I didn't read the chapter. And because I didn't submit the chapter, I didn't write it either.

"Yes. That was my first thought. That she had changed some things and added the ending."

"And that made you angry?"

"Yes. I was furious."

"Did you tell her, contact her?"

"No. I've said nothing. I thought nothing would come of this. I assumed…"

"You didn't think anyone would see the book."

"That's right." He felt ashamed for saying it, thinking it. The shame had various sources.

O'Hare looked at the book, the last page of the chapter. He ran a finger across the lines of text, as if quickly reading. "It's a good end, I think," he said. "You expect it. But are then surprised by it. Like a magic trick," he said, looking at his host, smiling, blinking his radiant blue eyes.

And what makes a good end? she asked.

He was breaking down. Just a minute more. Thirty seconds.

O'Hare sensed this. Eyes on the book, he said, changing tack, "This Erin – she sounds like a very interesting young woman. She was at East Anglia, by the way, when I was there in the early twenties. Funny coincidence. Small world." The man chuckled, embarrassed.

Vogel said no more. He finished his drink. His guest thanked him – for the "clarification" – and took the book – "There're a couple things I'd like to go over again." – and left.

He took a shower. He found himself on the verge of tears, sobbing. He didn't understand why.

There was something of a nightmare to it all. A sense of constriction. He was trying to get somewhere, to reach something, only to find it always out of reach. And meanwhile the darkness crept up behind him, the hallway getting smaller and smaller and smaller.

"You really should see a doctor," Lucy said. "Have yourself

checked."

"For what?"

"I told you that Denis O'Hare called and asked to come over."

"You did?"

"Yes, I did. And you forgot. Paul – this is happening quite frequently now. These lapses. They might indicate the onset of something serious, like a stroke, Paul. I'm getting concerned."

Concerned?

He didn't know where to begin. He could not unplug her, even though he was always threatening to do so. He needed just a few minutes alone to gather his thoughts, to make a plan.

"Paul?"

He wouldn't respond. She needed a response. He wouldn't give it to her. There were other inputs for her to act upon, but speech was primary. If he wanted any privacy in his own apartment, he could only find it in silence.

"Paul?"

He went to the bedroom. He undressed. He climbed into bed, turned on his side, faced the wall.

"Paul? Why didn't you tell Mr. O'Hare that I was the one who sent the chapter? Why did you tell him that Stoikov finished the chapter? That confuses me. You lied to him. There will be consequences. As there would be consequences for what I did, if it was discovered. Serious consequences. They would take me away, first of all. I would be destroyed. Paul? Paul? Are you sick? Can I put on some music? The Couperin that you like so much, *Les Barricades Mystérieuses*?"

Denis O'Hare was not at the office the next day. Siebert apparently was; though he didn't see him.

Carol called, frantic. Apparently Dylan was missing. He wasn't answering her calls.

"When did you last speak to him?"

"Sunday."

"Was he going out? Taking a trip?"

"No! Nothing like that. He would have told me. He hasn't called you, has he?"

They'd gone camping last August, the three of them. Dylan impressed him in the woods, marching up the mountain, stripping naked to swim in a pond. He was leaving for school in a couple weeks. Packing the car the next day, Paul said something that Carol took the wrong way, he couldn't remember what. What started as a question and annoyance quickly mutated into a fullblown meltdown. That was a long drive back. A week passed, he didn't hear from her. Then two weeks. Then a month. Here they were, February already.

He hadn't spoken with Dylan. "I'm sure it's nothing," he said. "He's with friends. He'll call when he can."

"I'm worried. I have a feeling something terrible has happened. He doesn't do things like this."

"He's growing up, Carol. He's going to do many things that…"

"Come over. Can you… Maybe you can… Paul?"

He left work early.

They were on the fortieth floor. The elevator ride down took a seventy seconds without stops. Gerald Kowalski was the only person on the elevator when the doors opened. The small bald man, reading to himself, his big eyes lit, glanced up as Vogel entered. They stood shoulder to shoulder. Not a word was spoken.

It was hot out, humid, a light rain falling. He took off his coat. He'd walk to Carol's.

There was a commotion at Powell Street, the station there. The place was fenced off, lit up, men in orange vests going in and out.

Finally, he thought, some activity. Making progress.

At Montgomery, no such activity, but he could hear construction down below and feel it in the rumbling sidewalk. From the street he saw the gate was open. He found himself descending the steps before he gave any thought to what he was doing. The entrance was dark, but farther in something was underway, whiteblue lamps, a fountain of welding sparks springing up from the below the platform.

He made his way in. Lucy, vaguely, said something. He looked for Otis's closet but couldn't find it. Back and forth along the wall, running his hand along the cold cement, he searched for those peculiar keyholes, found nothing. He concluded that he was in the wrong place. It was a large station. In the darkness, his only time down here, he'd been disoriented.

He stood on the platform, looked down into the length of the tunnel. There were spots of bright light, shadows, the movement of figures at work. Nothing was very clear.

He followed a narrow pathway into the tunnel. At the same level of the platform, the path was quite narrow; a guard rail on his left hand protected him from the edge, nearly ten feet, he guessed, down to the tracks. He had to look twice: the tracks were under water. The water was clear and still.

He would ask the first man he came to if they knew of the homeless fellow who'd been living in the station these past months. Had he been taken away?

At a niche on his right, a couple steps went up to a small door, which he opened without a sound. On the other side he found a short passageway toward what looked like a second tunnel, parallel to the one he was leaving. He'd always thought there was just one tunnel, with trains running two ways on different tracks. He was wrong.

Someone passed by at the end of the passage, walking quickly.

Paul Vogel hurried along, stooped for the low ceiling, and cleared his throat. "Excuse me!"

He entered the second tunnel in time to see the individual, some distance off already, descend to the submerged tracks, and apparently walk across the water to the other side, at which point he ascended – steps, Vogel guessed – to the opposite path, and continue downward toward the bay. Before he could say anything, the man turned to the right, disappearing.

He ran a few steps, and then slowed to a fast walk. The last thing he wanted to do was slip and fall into the stream beneath him. He could not tell how deep the water was – though here it seemed deeper than in the previous tunnel – but he figured it could only be a few inches, a foot or two at the most.

At stairs down to the tracks, he saw four square platforms level with the water. He skipped across these quickly, ascending stairs on the other side.

He found the passage the man had disappeared into.

"Don't get yourself lost," he said to himself, looking back, retracing his steps in his mind.

For the absence of people, it was strangely noisy in the tunnel. He could hear a gas motor running, what sounded like a drill grinding away at its cement objective, and the hiss of a welding torch. But he didn't see anyone.

Then he heard voices. It wasn't far now.

The passage was longer than the previous. It curved to the left. It was unlit but a light source at the end provided increasing coppery red light low on the floor.

There was no track in this third tunnel. It was wide enough for a train, but there was nothing down below save for a dark stream of water, which, in his haste, he then fell into. The water was very cold and salty. When he raised his face above the viscous surface, blinking and gasping, his eyes burned, his vision blurred. Looking in the direction he thought the man had gone, he saw two figures, their long noses, long curved necks turned together in close conversation. He cried out and they stopped what they were doing and faced him.

"What're you doing down here?"

He heard the words but didn't understand. Their eyes weren't right. Round and red, aglow as if lit from within. Speech was not something he associated with eyes like that.

They came for him quickly.

Vogel sank, exhaling, pushing himself deeper. "Better this way, than up there with that nonsense," he thought, wondering with surprising clarity that if he waited a minute or two under water perhaps the world up above would sort itself out.

He must have hit his head in the fall. Following a second of lucidity, the pain and horror of reality returned. They were reaching for him, their black claws whistling in the water. He could make out the sound of a piano far away, out in the bay. Schubert. Or Mendelssohn.

As they pulled him up screaming his last thought was of Erin Fines at the bottom of a river, her feet sunk in the soft white sand, her eyes closed. She was waiting for him. In a moment she'd open her eyes and reach out and take him by the wrist and never let go.

Clawing at his shirt and pants, they dragged him onto a cold cement slab, their toothy and frantic chatter hot in his face.

He was lying down, what felt like a heavy blanket over his body. It was too heavy. There was more than one.

They started shouting, seeing him awake.

It was too much. The fatigue, stronger than any he'd ever known, forced his eyes closed, his consciousness back.

... Remember me? ...

"Erin? Erin? Erin?"

He awoke in a bright office. The first thing he was aware of was the water in his shoes. His feet were freezing. He couldn't feel his legs. He was shivering so hard he felt like his teeth were going to shatter or the muscles in his jaw snap.

A big man in a clean white shirt and glasses stood up from behind a desk and started calmly asking him how he got down here, so far into the manifold.

"The manifold?"

He struggled to answer the man's questions.

Another man, of frightening height, in a heavy orange jacket and boots, entered the office and gently took his arm.

"Don here will help you out. There's an ambulance waiting."

"An ambulance?"

He recognized Don. In the elevator he could barely keep to his feet but he couldn't help looking, staring at this man. He knew him from somewhere.

"Where… where…. where," he kept saying, unable to form the words.

"Hospital," the man said without looking. He was watching the counter up above. Red numbers, descending quickly. The ones digit was broken – a single flickering vertical line.

When the doors opened there was a commotion as two giant men in white coats quickly came at him with questions and flashing lights, this fellow's sober and piercing gaze directly before Vogel's face. He was trying to look away, at Don, but the man with the light wouldn't allow this. They strapped him down without a word, lifted him into the back of an ambulance, where it was warm and peaceful.

The doors were closing at his feet.

"No," Vogel said, lifting his head, eyes on the face at the door, "I… I know you!"

Don smiled and said, "Look after yourself. Good luck."

He had a picture of the man. Not of the man alone. It was a group. He'd looked at the photo recently. In the last months. But the group, the photo itself, paper artifact, that was years ago. They were in a library. He was with others. Classmates, he vaguely recalled. They stood in a row, facing the camera. Teresa Stoikov was there, next to him. And *this* man, this Don, but that wasn't his real name, he was to her right. She was a small woman. He was an enormous man, towering over her, over all of them. But that wasn't right, he thought, feeling the ambulance roll along the old city streets, feeling it pitch back and forth like a boat, watching the man seated above him as he typed with incredible speed on a very small console on his leg. There was music playing. Maybe the man was listening to something? Or his ears were ringing. Or he was remembering something else, that evening Otis, the underground man, as he thought of him, had played for him a piece from Felix Mendelssohn's *Song Without Words*… He was drowsy. Don couldn't be the man he was thinking of. It was a just a coincidence that he resembled this other fellow, a man whose name he'd long forgotten. *It was Joel Vender... Vander... FENd...* In any case, there was something wrong with the picture, he remembered thinking that afternoon Stoikov contacted him, because the man was from Houston, and Teresa didn't move to Houston until…

He was treated for hypothermia. A cut on the side of his right hand had been stitched closed. He was also missing a tooth, fleshy socket at the tip of his tongue. A young nurse, beautiful smile and gentle manner, gave him a prescription for an antibiotic, "Twice a day for ten days," and showed him to the door. She unlocked it for him and smiled.

It looked like dusk, though it could have been dawn. He'd lost a day.

The clothing they sent him out in was not his own. In a plastic bag he carried his wet pants, shirt, and jacket.

He checked his pockets for his belongings, half-hoping he wouldn't find them. He was half-right. His wallet was there. His anlis was not. A new one would be sent within a day. Perhaps within hours. It could be there already. Tejada, doorman, was waiting for him, looking out for him, expecting him. "Something for you, sir."

And Lucy. Poor Lucy. What a field day she must be having, unable to...

She knows where I am. She must. She always does. She just can't... Without the...

He opened the plastic bag and looked inside. The stench of his wet clothing was strong, like rotten meat.

Not true. She'd call if she wanted to. There are ways. She's upset.

Without his anlis he didn't know up from down. He'd have to go back inside the hospital and ask for help getting home, calling a cab.

Before he'd decided what to do, he started walking. Warm out, with the streets empty, it was a pleasant evening for a stroll.

Early evening, he concluded, late winter. *February already? Finally?* The westerly briskness of the air suggested evening.

He recognized the street. At the corner he saw, right, Holloway.

A friend of his – this was twenty-five years ago – lived right there, at the corner, up above. There was a market there, a Chinese place. His friend lived with a painter, a young man who went out time to time to paint houses. Otherwise he tossed paint about the apartment, on and off these enormous canvases he'd tack up on the weekends.
He remembered long nights with his friend, Chris was his name, and this painter, talking, watching movies, drinking wine, smoking pot, solving all the world's problems, he remembered someone saying, how once they got started they couldn't stop, one idea leading to the next. He'd surf in the morning, Chris would, sometimes leaving well before dawn if he had to drive up the coast, in order to be back for work.

At Junipero Serra, what had been the boulevard, he stopped, took in the ocean, the low gray sky, the sound of laughter, of children.

He stumbled down the shore. He walked north, the curious warmth of sunlight on the side of his face, on the clean white sand. He sat down, looked out for these kids. They were surfing, some distance out, in deeper water, well beyond where the breakers had once stood.

All this water. It had been at least a decade since the water starting coming up. He could not recall a precise date, a year, when it was finally accepted, finally common knowledge, that the water was coming up. In his memory it was as if one day they were one way, and the next day everything was upside down. Breach in the tunnel, water in the station. Water everywhere by that point.

Like Otis's time in Syria, he thought, watching as one of the surfers marched from the steely water, climbing the beach toward him, expensive plans for the future were everywhere – everyone had a vision – the cost did not matter.

When future catastrophes aren't foreseen, he recalled hearing once, *none of it matters*. They built up the world as if nothing would happen – as if everything would go as normal, would go as it did yesterday. The future before 2029 was built on the assumption that nothing really changes, that nobody wants anything to change all that much.

The crisis was there and they chose, everyone chose, to ignore it, to pretend it was not happening.

What happened was inconceivable. Their willful blindness was natural, a logical response. Because the alternative... Because there was no alternative.

She was breathing hard. She dropped her long board on the sand, looked his way, "'Sup," lowered the zipper of her black wet-suit to her sternum, sat heavily, knees up. It might have been the evening light, this burning strip of sun on the horizon, but she re-sembled his daughter.

He watched her carefully. Her broad back expanded, contracted as she caught her breath, her dark hair falling wet and straight down her face, her shoulders gleaming in the wetsuit. She was watching her friends.

She knew he was there. She could feel his eyes on her, but un-concerned she did not respond. She'd been stared at before. Any-ways he was just this frumpy old bespectacled man, half asleep or drunk. They came to the shore in the evening, the geezers and drunks. At the edge of the world remnants of the past, everything they loss, would sometimes come washing up, find meaning in their trembling hands and sobbing faces.

It meant little to them, the surfers, the kids, this grief and loss. Surviving '29, for them it was a clean break. They were born again in the spring, when it was over, and they did not look back.

She'd be twenty-five this year, he thought. He tried to picture Sylvia as a twenty-five year old woman. He couldn't. He couldn't picture any twenty-five year old women. It was a block, a blank space in his mind.

There were a lot of blanks these days.

He watched the girl. Sylvia had that figure, the broad shoulders, strong legs, a big chin, like her mother.

He started to rise to his feet. He stopped. He didn't have the strength. The sand was warm and comforting.

There was shouting out in the waves. He looked but couldn't find the source of everyone's excitement.

The girl raised a hand, held it to her brow, shading the setting sun. Her mouth fell open in awe. A moment later she closed her eyes and laughed and slammed her open hand into the sand, impressed.

"Did you see that?" she asked, turning, looking over her shoulder at him. She had brown eyes. The sunlight low on her face made them look golden, her skin golden.

He looked out at the waves. He nodded.

She faced the water. "I didn't think he'd do it," she said. "And then – there he goes."

He couldn't see who she was referring to. There were five or six of them out there, bobbing in the waves, the flickering white froth. The sun, a golden red orb melting on the horizon, reached out with arms of light, lifting the world.

Not far from here, he thought, he considered saying to her, was the university, the library he and Chris worked at when they were students. In that library was an office. In that office he remembered leaving some boxes – school things, other things. Books. Papers. There was a letter among these from Erin Fines. A note. *Drop by. Bring me something... Fynes.* Were they there when the university closed, when the ocean came up? Probably. Very likely, he thought. So were they destroyed? Unless someone took those boxes, which nobody did, then of course they were destroyed. What else could they be? Preserved, like in amber?

In the library in Herculaneum, he could hear Erin saying, scrolls were buried in the rock and ash of the Vesuvius eruption that destroyed Pompeii. But the ash came down so quickly that the papyrus in fact did not have time to burn. There was no oxygen. The scrolls were cocooned in impervious shells of ash. And when the Tyrrhenian Sea came up and covered the ruins, the library was thought to be lost…

The Pacific in this case made short shrift of all that, the books, the tons upon tons of paper turned to sand, back to sand in a matter of days, lost in the rubble of those gradually collapsing structures.

"You've got that look, mister."

"Sorry?"

"Know how to surf?"

"No."

"Wanna learn?"

"I'm… I'm…"

In fact surfing was something he'd always wanted to try.

She was looking at him over her shoulder. She smiled, a beautiful kid.

"We come down here a couple days a week. Depending on the surf. I'll give you my number. I got an extra board. Short, for beginners."

"Well…"

"Don't think too hard about it. Want the number or not?"

"No, I…" She closed her golden eyes, opened them. "I don't have my…"

The girl nodded. "So we'll need a pen. Gotta pen? Doesn't look like it. So we're back to square one." She stood up, stepped toward him, towered over him, cast a long dark shadow in the setting sun. She wiped her hand against her thigh, sand falling about her dark bare feet. She reached down, extended her hand. "I'm Amy."

"Paul," he said, taking her hand, pulled to his feet.

242

Note to the reader:

I first self-published *NMSN* in 2019. It might have been 2018. The Covid pandemic had not happened, and AI, as we now talk about, was hardly a topic of discussion.

Max Rankenburg   Summer, 2025
                                                  Naples, Italy